For Sam & Suzanne ~

the latest production of

your cousin, my brother —

With love,

R Saul Jansson

(& Hilly too!)

THE DEVIL'S LAUGH AND OTHER STORIES

H. Alan Tansson

Illustrated by
John Fries Mitchell and the author

iUniverse, Inc.
New York   Bloomington

iUniverse books may be ordered through booksellers or by contacting:

iUniverse
1663 Liberty Drive
Bloomington, IN 47403
www.iuniverse.com
1-800-Authors (1-800-288-4677)

ISBN: 978-1-4401-6066-0 (sc)
ISBN: 978-1-4401-6067-7 (ebook)
ISBN: 978-1-4401-6068-4 (dj)

Printed in the United States of America

iUniverse rev. date: 12/29/2009

Also by H. Alan Tansson:
We Think We Think. Captions for the Cartoons We Live: Volume I. iUniverse Press. 2010, and *Antidisestablishmentarianistically Speaking. Captions to the Cartoons We Live Volume 2.* iUniverse Press 2010.

To Carol Whitman (1948–1963), who was the Perfect's sister and the Weaver's aunt.

"Good horseshoe nails are always good nails, but what is good in literature is all a matter of taste. There is no standard. You like it because you like it, and if certain other people praise a thing it is a good reason why you should let it severely alone—or buy it. It all depends upon who this person is."

—Elbert Hubbard, "On Advertising Books" in *A Message to Garcia and Thirteen Other Things*. The Roycrofters, East Aurora, NY, 1901.

Contents

Acknowledgments

Many thanks to Sarah and Ken Miller, who have given me permission to use art from the notebooks of my late friend, John Fries Mitchell, of Maple Shade, New Jersey. John's work adorns the cover and the story "The Devil's Laugh." All other art is my own. Thanks also to John R. Krueger, *bakhshi*, who did the first edit and caught all the embarrassing errors.

Adventures of a Cameo Merchant

Translated from the original Albigensian
and as retold by H. Alan Tansson

The Conch and the Cameo-Maker

Once upon a time there was a boy who lived alone with his mother by the sea. He never traveled anywhere, nor even set foot in a boat, but supported his mother by swimming to the oyster beds and diving for pearls. Merchants would come and supply him and his mother with everything they needed in return for the pearls. However, the two needed very little beyond what they grew in their garden, which was olives and onions and garlic, and chickens that lived on all sorts of seeds.

Naturally, like any other young boy, he dreamt of becoming a merchant and traveling the world to gather what he could of its experience in trade for his talents, and having a good time at it besides. He was born with three great talents, which his mother told him were all related. The first of these was the ability to dive very deep beneath the surface of the sea to find small treasures. And he had learned to hold his breath so long when he dove for pearl oysters that people in town nicknamed him "the Breath," which his mother told him was his greatest blessing.

The second of his skills was the talent to find pictures in nearly anything. He saw animals in clouds and faces in the shadows of the sea cliffs. He could scratch the surface of the most common things to bring out the pictures in them. Indeed,

3

he could draw beautiful images on stones and carve any sort of thing you might wish. Whenever he was lucky enough to find a conch, he would bring it up instead of oysters. By making a cameo from a conch shell he could get more from the merchants than they would pay for a whole bucket of pearls, which were very common in those parts.

His third talent was his greatest passion. He loved riddles. His mother told him that this talent was the combination of the other two, which was a riddle he could not solve. She also said it would be the end of him. But the boy didn't worry too much about what his mother said, because she was always talking.

One day when he was about to dive down to the oyster beds, he saw what appeared to be a large pink conch moving slowly across the sea floor. As he rarely saw conchs, and had never seen one so big, he took a very deep breath, and with a surge of joy in his veins swam down to retrieve the giant conch.

It was so very heavy it took all his strength to swim with only one hand. Oysters fit in the pouch tied around his waist, but not a conch such as this one. He ran out of breath before he got to the surface and let go of the conch as he began to pass out. In this way he saved himself and made it to the surface with the last ounce of his strength.

Gasping for breath, he pondered his problem, for he was resolved to have the conch. From it he could make cameos for kings and princes, and with such a treasure he would surely be able to become a merchant and leave this life. So he dove again, only this time he simply swam with the conch a short distance and dropped it closer to shore. In this way, after diving many times, he was able to bring the giant conch to the shallows.

He took it home and prepared their largest kettle full of boiling water and threw the conch in. After boiling an hour, the conch did not fall from its shell. When it had cooled the boy reached in the shell to pull it out and felt it pull back, as if it were still alive. So he filled the shell with pure white salt to take the liquid from the conch and kill it overnight.

The next morning with his knife he began to carefully etch the outside of the shell into hexagons the size of the cameos he would make. This way, when he struck the shell with a rock, it would break into perfect pieces. But as he was scratching the first line into the shell's surface, a sound came from the inside of the shell. It sounded like a voice.

"What do you think you are doing there?"

The boy almost didn't believe himself, but he responded as if it were quite normal to speak to a conch. "I am inscribing you to make the most marvelous cameos for the king. That is what I am doing."

The small head of a large snail pushed through the salt in the shell. "That is just nonsense. Put me down."

But the boy persisted. "If you would please leave your shell, I could make cameos for the king and make enough fortune to become a merchant."

The conch replied, "That is nonsense. I should think you can make more from me just as I am."

At which point, the boy, thinking himself a great one for riddles, put the conch down and sat on a stone and thought.

"You can't be killed, and now you speak my language. Are you perhaps a god?"

"Do I look like I could create heaven and earth?" the snail replied. "Of course I am no god!"

"But you're no ordinary conch, either," replied the boy. "What can you do that I can make more from you as you are?"

"Why, I believe I can see the future and possibly make it happen," said the conch. "I'm not at all sure, but just a moment ago I saw that you would try to break my shell, and I felt I could make it turn out otherwise, which is why I said what I just did."

"I find this very odd," said the boy. "You are not a god, but speak and do things of this sort."

"Forgive me, but I knew yesterday you would dive to get me, and so I thought you might lose your breath. Didn't it come true as I thought?"

"Yes," the boy responded. "But I got you nevertheless."

"Very true, but who is still holding onto his shell?"

The boy winced at that.

"Can you make miracles happen? Can you turn those stones into gems, for example, or can you fly?"

The conch twisted slightly toward the stones.

"I don't believe I can make stones into gems. But I have never tried to fly, living under water as I do. I shall give it a try."

Then the conch retreated into his shell and a bubbling, gurgling noise echoed from within. He rose almost imperceptibly off the ground, but enough that the boy's mouth dropped open. Then the shell dropped and the gurgling stopped, and the sound of wheezing and coughing replaced it, just as if the conch were an old man.

The boy was very impressed and took pity on the ancient conch. He gently picked it up and carried it to the fish pond in his mother's garden.

...but I have never tried to fly, living under water as I do.

6

It didn't take long for the story of the conch to spread from the neighborhood to the countryside, and through merchants to far-off lands. So before a week had passed the boy and his mother were besieged by local pilgrims, and soon thereafter by messengers of kings and wise men seeking the conch's oracle.

Just as the conch said, the two were able to become quite wealthy by leaving the conch in his shell, charging just pennies to let people line up for his opinions on things.

Soon the boy had grown to be a young man who was as skillful with a sword as he had once been in holding his breath. People now nicknamed him "Flash," because he could defend the conch from anyone who tried to steal this valuable treasure.

One day a powerful king sent a squadron of ships across the sea, and landed a mounted guard at a beach not far from the garden in order to steal the conch and place him in a temple in his capital, to make it a famous and thriving center of trade. The young man went to the conch for the very first advice he had ever asked it, and the conch responded, "Don't worry, I believe I was once good at this sort of thing."

Immediately the mounted guard was buried by a rock slide from the cliff, and a wind blew up that threw the king's fleet into the rocks along the shore.

"Our friend and benefactor is a god, and not simply an oracle!" the young man's mother cried out.

The conch chuckled.

"After spending so much time giving advice to people, I remembered that I was once the god of the conchs and had powers like this. It was quite necessary, for they would have killed you and put me in a temple, or made a reliquary out of me."

"Thank you!" said the young man. "You have saved our lives."

"And you have saved mine," said the conch. "For I might never have remembered who I once had been were it not for you. A god does not always get to stay a god, if he lets his subjects forget him. I think I got sidetracked years ago."

"After that display you should have subjects again," said the young man.

"I think so, if you would be so kind as to let me return to the sea, which has been my real home for many thousands of years."

The young man looked expectantly at his mother, who put her head down to show it was her son's decision.

"I will of course return you to the sea, after you tell me what I need to know before setting on my way. For I have been longing to see the world just as you've been longing to return to the sea."

"I could have gone at any moment," the conch mused. "Only I promised to help you when we were first introduced, and you didn't cut my shell into cameos"

"My mother has enough to live the rest of her days, and I have saved just enough to start my trade," the young man said.

"Before I go back to the sea I should give you a boon or at least some advice, for I've already seen such human misery and falsehood in your garden, it's a riddle beyond this snail's understanding. But then, I must say I understand slugs.

"I have given counsel to villains who wanted revenge on the children of their enemies, who spoke of plucking out eyes and burning traitors. There is so little I understand of people; but I gave them advice that they might hang without ever thinking to curse my oracle. At least I understand slugs.

"I have given counsel to lovers who would have their rivals poisoned and wished to know how to do it without being caught. I cannot fathom why they came to me, a sea-snail, for advice. I gave them advice that got them seduced by someone else, to leave their love to their rivals. It's helpful to understand slugs.

"I have given secret counsel to poor slaves who came with their masters. Boys and girls sold into bondage by rich parents for a bauble, who endured the most ugly fantasies of the most ugly men until they became ugly themselves. I have shown them the path of courage to die with grace and dignity, to become free. But I have shown their masters the way to the dung heap. I cannot for the life of me understand these things, but this is what I did. I simply understand slugs.

"I have been asked by the scribes of simpletons to help devise dungeons that would amplify the unending screams of tortured souls in the waiting rooms of innocents being made to confess implausible crimes. I have given them fantastic plans to haunt their dreams so they would die of fright in their sleep before returning home. Don't they know that two can play at escargot?

"But even worse are the pious hermits who have come to ask the opinion of a snail, claiming they would not do unto others what they would not have done to themselves. Yet I hear them lie to themselves in every other sentence, pronouncing things they don't believe but wish to hear with their own ears. Even the best of people give themselves permission to lie and cheat each other in righteousness. I give them counsel to do as they say and not as they believe, but do they understand me? I doubt it. It is a shame more people don't understand slugs.

"But now I must give you my counsel, for I have seen you take good care of your mother.

"Your talents are as your mother said, for you are good at diving deep below the surface of things, just as you are good at finding beauty at the surface. But you were not so good at riddles up to now as your mother thought, and I shall give you the help you need, because you are sure to encounter many riddles in your life and will have a few adventures doing it."

Then the young man's mother began to cry, for she knew her son was going to leave and she'd never see him again.

"Your son will always be thinking of you," the conch said to his mother. "And don't worry. For I will give him a gift which is especially for you. This sort of thing is usually done with pearls, but because he is so talented, a piece of my shell will do even better."

Saying this, the conch reached down to the earth below him, lifted up his shell and threw it down by its corner onto a rock, breaking off a large chunk of his glistening shell.

"Your son will carve his image into this piece of my shell, which you can look at to see him as he grows older for the rest of your life." And with that the giant conch began to slide himself over the ground toward the beach.

Now it was the young man who sat crying, as his mother picked up their old friend, the oracle, and placed him tenderly in the water by the sea. As he disappeared beneath the surface, the young man and his mother went into their house and went to sleep.

The next morning when they awoke there were no pilgrims, for the way had been blocked by the rockslide, and a silly rumor began that the oracle was a sea-god who had made a tornado and disappeared into the sky.

When the young man and his mother looked down at the beach, however, they were in time to see three ancient discarded conch shells on the sand, and three naked sea-snails crawling back into the sea to their own comfortable shells beneath the waves.

The young man yelled his thanks as he ran to retrieve these wonderful treasures, which he immediately began carving into precious cameos for princes and kings. At the end of a year, he finally finished, and carved his own image on the oracle's shell as a gift to his mother.

He left her then, and traveled to all the most famous fairs, slowly selling his beautiful cameos for the best prices in gold and silks and spices and all the other things that merchants dealt with in those days.

In just a year he owned several trains of camels and had hired a small army to defend his goods on his trips, until he was wealthy enough to build a villa for himself that was, with his army of friends and helpers and their families, no less than a small city with gardens and barns for herds of livestock, and festivals and a temple where folks could set up sanctuaries to their gods.

He did all this, and thrived and studied and was well-loved for many years, until one day he realized that he had traded all his talents and what he loved and did best, all for something that he thought, as a boy, he wanted.

Thus it was that the merchant gave away everything he had to his friends and their families. All except a donkey. For he still longed to go out into the world and dive deep beneath the surface of things, while looking closely at the surface of things to see what could be made of it. He wanted to do this simply to solve those riddles concerning people in all their ugliness. For his oracle the sea-snail had said he could not understand people, but that he understood slugs very well. And while this seems a very simple thing to say, it can still be quite a riddle.

And so the young man of our story, whom we first met as a boy, was now a prosperous man of middle age. It was this man, known to all as simply "the Cameo Merchant," who set out to start his life anew.

The Riddle of the Sphincter

It took several months, but after meeting hundreds of other merchants and wanderers from everywhere on the globe, our friend the cameo merchant discovered the location of the most famous riddle in those days. He had heard stories even as a small boy about a great snake called the Sphincter that let none pass who could not solve its riddle.

After many questions and even more bribes, the man discovered that the great snake guarded a small and unlikely path through the fenlands that many lone travelers took, preferring to face the Sphincter than death by gangs of thieves who camped by all the main roads. For all roads through the miles of bogs led to a famous thieves' market, where no one, not even a thief, was safe coming in ones or twos.

As he rode back and forth around the bogs looking for this small path, the man asked himself again why he was going to such trouble, and reminded himself that his purpose in life was now to find riddles to solve.

Finally, he noticed a dip in the side of the road and saw a break in the ferns and cattails below him. Perhaps this was the entrance to the Sphincter's path.

As he turned his donkey down the slope and into a break in the briars, he began thinking it over again. This riddle might come with a high price, for the Sphincter squeezed its victims to death, crushing all the bones in their bodies and leaving the dead with only their head. And then the man remembered his mother's words, that he should find his end chasing riddles, and he briefly shuddered.

He sat upright, resolved to forget any fears, because, after all, he had lived a wonderful life thus far, and wished only to understand the riddle of life's ugliness. He was helped in this resolve when he saw that the path was well-traveled. He passed several horse droppings that could not be more than a few days old, if that. Not only that, but they came from several different horses. Apparently this was just another little-known path to the thieves' market. Unless the answer to the Sphincter's riddle had become well-known, this couldn't be the path to the great snake. He might expect an ambush by one or two thieves at most; nothing he couldn't handle—for no large caravans worth a whole gang would cross the fenlands this way.

Thinking these kinds of thoughts, and preparing himself for an ambush for several miles, he was not at all surprised when a bandit leapt on him from a large blood-stained boulder, hoping to slit the merchant's throat. But this was child's play for the merchant, who had defended the oracle for many years, learning his moves and tricks from the best.

"Your sign hardly needs repainting," he said as he ran the highwayman through. "But we shall give it a fresh coat."

Then he sat the thoughtless thief down against the boulder to let the vultures clarify the rock's message.

Not long after, the path came to a slight rise above a fork in the road. The merchant now saw something very large gliding to the middle of the path as he approached, perhaps thirty paces away. It was not another ambush, nor a robber at all.

He stopped and it stopped. While he couldn't make out its shape, it seemed about the size of a cow, which is very big indeed for something in the middle of a marsh. In the sun it was glistening a dozen hues of the brightest blue.

Amazed and excited, the merchant got off his donkey, but the moment his feet touched the ground a filthy skull came bouncing toward him, and his donkey bolted into the bogs braying at the top of her lungs.

Seeing the skull, he winced, for the tales were indeed true. He had, in fact, found the right path, and the great snake that took its name from the sphincter muscle in our body which squeezes out our filth. But a stench covered the skull gently rolling off the road by his feet, and as the merchant took a deep breath from the opposite direction he considered whether our muscle got its name from the Sphincter instead of the other way around.

Holding his breath while deciding what to do, the man watched the creature begin to uncoil. Just then his donkey's braying was cut short with a squealing and silence, and he was glad he'd gotten off. The Sphincter's children were said to live in the bogs on either side, to make short shrift of anything that ran away. The Sphincter gave you a chance to choose life or death by asking its riddle. To face this riddle and solve it had been one of his childhood ambitions, and because he knew that several others had gotten through the crossroads to tell their tale, the merchant knew there was chance of success. Here he was, at last.

The Sphincter's tail ended in the body of a squat little man, and like the tail of a rattlesnake it warned intruders to back off. It was this tail that had bowled the dirty skull down the road. The man-rattle had only arms, belly, and legs. But out of his middle came the end of the monster's tail looking just like a large male organ, nearly twice as big as that little man's body.

Sometimes he dragged this tail-tip along with two hands, flailing it and waving it about. Other times it stiffened, becoming the tail of the giant Sphincter itself, lifting the man-rattle's feet off the ground and taking him where it willed, much as any man's tool is said to do.

The merchant was transfixed by this spectacle. Meanwhile, the squat headless man's body was hopping in front of the Sphincter like a frog, holding a skull on its shoulders where its head should have been.

Stifling a laugh, the merchant remembered he had worries enough on his own shoulders, for the glistening blue scales behind the man-rattle had begun sliding silently toward him.

Meanwhile, little old man-rattle put down the skull that had lately served as his head. He squatted on it and let out a steaming whoosh, like a cow lifting its tail. Then he grabbed his limp tail like a croquet mallet and swatted the steaming skull right at the merchant.

The merchant deftly moved out of the way and sighed with relief.

The headless little man lined up another shot and the merchant jumped again. But he was being tricked, for the eyes that lined up the shot were now at his side. He had jumped closer to the Sphincter.

The third shot came close behind him, and the merchant jumped again, but instead of breathing a sigh of relief, he gasped as he realized his error. He had unwittingly jumped into a silky curtain of golden hair and stood only an arm's length from a wall of blue scales.

He looked up, and the giant Sphincter was swaying directly above him, looking down.

The stories told of the Sphincter said that whether you were man, woman, or beast, its face was so beautiful you couldn't take your eyes from it. Indeed, the merchant found himself confronted by the prettiest face he could imagine. For the Sphincter had the head of a goddess with a glowing hood of soft copper hair that flowed around its victim like a fountain, as her liquid eyes softened her victim's nerves.

To meet with the Sphincter was a trial for anyone, man or woman. Its eyes would reach inside its victim, holding the poor soul transfixed while its tongue slipped into an ear to speak the riddle. And so, with the person dazed and immobilized, its tail would molest them from behind.

With a giant snake tickling one's ear with its tongue and one's bottom with its tail, no one could concentrate on a riddle. But for the merchant, to wager his life on his skill at riddles was his oldest fantasy.

He suddenly heard a beautiful voice whispering melodious words into his head. But for the merchant, each word of the riddle announced itself like a trumpet:

"What has *no* shape and *all* shapes and none can bear to live with?"

Merchants everywhere can hold onto their wits as they bargain and bluff over the most seductive business deals; and merchants in this part of the world were used to the roving hands of barbarian guides and camel drivers. Without another thought, he kicked the tail away as he closed his eyes and covered his ears to better ponder the question.

The snake's question is difficult, yet all in all there are perhaps three dozen skulls that the tail kicks about. A dozen travelers pass this way each month—for I have already noted how frequently the road is traveled. Over the years there must have been thousands who have passed through safely. In fact it is probably the favorite path of thieves, who know they have nothing to fear.

This, he thought, *is the* real *riddle. For thieves know the answer, which is that they have nothing to worry about if they answer wrong, or merely anything they can think of. I have just proven it is those who guess the riddle* correctly *who are crushed to death!*

He held his breath as he repeated the riddle to himself: "What has no shape and all shapes and none can bear to live with?"

A strategy was running through his head. "I could say 'death,' or 'love,' or 'hunger,' which are surely not correct—and so I would live. Is this what I came for, simply to pass this test as every thief has passed before me?

"Certainly the idea of such a riddle—a riddle of life such that those who guess the answer shall be squeezed to death—this would be a horrible and shapeless truth that none can bear to live with."

He longed to look into the Sphincter's eyes, as he smelled its hair washing over his face and ears.

Why not answer "longing," he thought, *and be done with this, for the Sphincter has given me a longing to give up this quest for truth.*

He heard the Sphincter whisper its riddle again softly, and as he began to swoon his eyes fluttered open. Its tongue suggested that he open them wider, to see the riddle in the Sphincter's eyes with its most perfect answer, and thus he was reminded to close them all the tighter. Then he thought of screaming out, "My longing for the Sphincter has all shapes and no shape and I cannot bear to live with it." Indeed this seemed the very answer to the fabulous riddle, but as he heard his mouth begin to utter this truth he heard the voice of any thief, the commonest slug calling out such an answer, for this was the most obvious thought to come to any of its victim's minds.

Suddenly he heard a voice inside him ask yet again, "What kind of truth would destroy those who would guess it?" for this, indeed, was the nature of the real riddle, and certainly its answer.

At the same time, the merchant heard a tremendous whoosh and perceived a drastic change come over reality, as the perfume of excrement overtook his excitement and longing.

With a triumphant yell he exclaimed, "What a remarkable load of crap! Why, *this* is the kind of truth that would destroy anyone!"

Drawing his sword with one hand he leapt at the Sphincter's tail and impaled it to the dirt screaming, "Both Truth and Crap have no shape and all shapes, and no one can bear to live with either of them!"

Pulling out his skinning knife with his other hand, he slit the snake from stern to gullet yelling, "Those who say they can't live with crap can't accept the truth: that we must live with it! But to accept that truth will destroy us if we don't fight it to the end for the sake of our souls."

And because the Sphincter's beautiful head was totally caught up in itself, hearing only the sweet nothings it whispered into the ears of its victims until it chose to release them, the head was still at his shoulders when he sliced it off with a clean sweep of his sword and rolled it, its entrails, and the twitching, ugly, dirty tail into the bog to rot.

Then, so as not to deprive the next traveler of a riddle, he made two crude signs as a memorial, and placed one at each path. The signpost to the left said, "Guess Wrong. Live Long!"

On the signpost to the right was written, "A head with no head on a tail on tails no longer."

After a prayer of thanks, the merchant picked up his bag (which had fallen from the donkey's back) and continued on his way to the right.

Here ends the story of the Merchant and the Sphincter, which I know you have never heard before. It's a secret story hated by the guardians of every truth that was ever proclaimed.

For the crossroads is still there, and one of the Sphincter's beautiful children is there to tantalize the unwary and ask its riddle. But few people brag about being there, for they wish to keep their seduction at the crossroads a secret. This is unfortunate, since history constantly reminds us that vicious fights break out between those jealous of their knowledge of the answer—the thief's answer—and their secret longing to keep the Sphincter for themselves.

He closed his eyes and covered his ears to better ponder the question.

The Riddle of All Riddles

Late that afternoon the merchant arrived at his destination. It was that town famous for its thieves' market. Everything there was sold by bandits in tradesmen's clothing—they were all robbers and conniving cutthroats.

You probably wonder why the merchant would come all this way to a thieves' market. First of all, he came to find the Sphincter, of which we have already told. But he didn't turn back after accomplishing that mission, because he also wished to see this market.

The reason he continued to this destination is that he thought he might find many old relics made of shells, which very few considered valuable. It is not that he needed money or trade, but he loved the thought of beautiful old shells to carve into cameos, and these would always be a passion for him. As a young man he could dive for his own shells, but as he grew old, this was no longer possible. Cameo-making was a good hobby to have as he wandered the world looking for riddles he might solve. In the thieves' market he knew he'd find many old articles made of large shells, such as broken oil lamps and fancy camel buckles, which he could have at low prices and carry safely away.

Arriving at the market he was overjoyed to see a riddle above its entrance:

"Bury your quarrels or you must bury your quarrels."

He was reading this when he noticed another riddle just below it, for an old beggar was sitting next to a box, crying, "End my life! Put an end to my misery, and inherit my treasures!"

This is a riddle, the merchant thought, *for in a marketplace full of cutthroats and brigands, one would think it an easy thing to trade a treasure for your life.*

"Peace be with you," said the merchant to a passing ruffian. "Tell me, why has no one killed that fellow over there?"

The bandit laughed, drew his sword, and pointed it at the sign above him. "Whoever you kill here you must dispose of. It is the only law we keep. No one wants to take the trouble to bury him, but to watch *your* head fly would be worth the trouble!" The bandit's blade flickered just above the merchant's shoulder, who parried the blow, for only a fine swordsman would dare enter a thieves' market.

My hands are the image of the riddle of all riddles!

"I should have guessed." He smiled at the would-be cutthroat. "But what about that treasure of his?"

The fellow laughed again. "Twice I've watched someone slice him open. They buried him in the dung heap and took his box of treasure. It was oily rags. In a week he was back with a new box."

"Darnedest dung heap!" exclaimed the merchant. "Must be some pretty strong crap."

"You want to try it out?" laughed the robber, his blade dancing once again.

The merchant stepped aside and bowed, taking the bandit's leave, for he knew he had discovered something nearly as strange as the Sphincter, and he was anxious to see how he might fare with the old man.

He walked over to him and reached for the box.

"Can I look at your treasure before I take the trouble to kill you?"

The beggar grabbed the chest to his chest. "I would kill you first, young man!" he clucked. Nevertheless, the old beggar took the lid from the box and the glare of the setting sun reflected on so many gems the merchant had to turn away. "Put me out of my misery and this treasure is yours."

The merchant bowed low and left.

Several days later he returned, disguised as an old witch with a basket of poisoned figs.

"Here old man," he cackled. "Have some of my figs to take the pain of your belly away."

The old man took the basket and sucked the figs down whole.

"We shall see if my magic can do the trick," chuckled the witch—who was, of course, the merchant in disguise.

The beggar threw open his robes to show a mass of scars and festering wounds. "See the pain in my belly," he exclaimed, "and pray your magic works!"

The merchant threw off his disguise. "I know you are a

great sorcerer who has discovered the secret of immortality. I can end your life and dispose of your riddle as I did the Sphincter's."

"What riddle?" the sorcerer whined. The merchant sat down by his side and said, "You fashioned a spell thinking the greatest riddle in life was to conquer death. And now, your reverence for power and knowledge has left you longing for powerlessness and death. Now *this* riddle is the greatest riddle of life, and you can't bear it any longer. When you discover a riddle to take the place of this one, old man, the curse of your spell will be broken."

"Wonderfully put," sighed the sorcerer. "For I can think of no greater riddle than myself, and it has been that way for centuries. I am very, very tired."

The merchant stood up, wrapped himself in his robes, and with a deep and theatrical voice, said, "The poison is working in your belly as we speak, and so I will tell you 'The Riddle of All Riddles,' and if you can solve it, you shall break the spell that has kept you alive for so long."

And with that, the merchant held up his hands to the sky, and chanted (as deeply as he could):

"It has many fingers to point with, but can only grasp a paradox."

The old sorcerer started to laugh through his pain, "Why that is the silliest riddle I've ever heard! It's much too simple. I'm a wizard with riddles! The answer is 'a riddle.'"

But then the old man's eyes opened wide and he wheezed, "You have outwitted me! It is not a *harder riddle* than all the rest, but the riddle *about* all riddles. Why, you really have discovered the riddle of all riddles, haven't you?"

Then the old man held up his hands and stretched out his fingers.

"Yes, yes—it is even these hands, which cast my spells. My hands are the image of the riddle of all riddles, and now another great hand stretches over them, its fingers touching mine in many directions. It is the Hand of Death!"

The sorcerer's brow stretched back as he made the face of a spell-maker, proclaiming:

"Witch-ever-Merchant, you've proved my riddle liddle."

This small bit of wit took on cosmic proportions for the old sorcerer, as he began to chuckle, and couldn't stop giggling until he gasped and expired with a broad smile on his face.

The merchant tenderly wrapped him up in the witch's cloak. He purchased a donkey from the attendant nearby, and carried the beggar and his box to a small orchard, where he dug the final resting place of the oldest beggar on earth. When he opened the box, it was still full of jewels and gemstones, and not oily rags. The old sorcerer had kept his promise and more, for at the bottom of the box was a little book with his most important spells written out quite legibly in longhand.

The Quarry of Suffering

The merchant sat down and thought, for now he had less need than ever to earn his living as a merchant. For years he'd heard of a fabled place called "the Quarry of Suffering," which dug itself, leaving gems strewn across its floor. He decided he'd become so good at riddles, he'd get to the bottom of this one, too. He wandered from market to market for many months asking about this miraculous quarry. One day, a camel driver said, "Anxious to air out your bones, brother? We leave several fools there every trip and we've never picked one up."

Several weeks later the caravan left the merchant and five other adventurers at the path to the Quarry of Suffering. They walked silently, apart from one another, and reached the quarry's edge at dusk. A vast emptiness spread out to the horizon and vultures soared below. The sky was gray-blue and blackness buried the bottom of the quarry.

Each man took his own place along the precipice. As they lit their fires to wait for morning, an orange crescent moon began to rise above the horizon. It became larger and larger, seeming to come toward them. One of the adventurers became afraid and began to run away. As he did, the ground gave way, and his screams were lost in the thunder of a landslide; and whether he was crushed in the darkness, no one could say—for no one heard the rocks reach the bottom.

The orange moon was a globe of silk as large as the dome of a mosque. It floated in the air above the quarry. Beneath it was a large basket with torches and a man in an orange caftan. He stopped the glowing moon at the precipice where the adventurers stood, and he addressed them:

"You are invited by the Perfect to the Quarry of Suffering. Whenever a living thing is made to suffer, emptiness consumes a bit of this quarry. The earth and clay that was someone's footing is no longer there; but a bit of gold dust, a gem or a nugget remains to pay for the suffering.

"You have come for these jewels—but you shall find only one—the Jewel of Perfect Justice. You must bring it to the Perfect to adorn its throne. If you fail this test, you will simply end your life of suffering."

The merchant spoke up. "I did not come to find precious stones, for I have enough of them. I came to solve the riddle of the quarry, which you have now explained. So tell me—if I find this jewel for your master, what do I gain by it?"

"Pure and perfect justice, of course," the man in the orange caftan replied with a sly wink. "Whoever wishes to take on this quest must come along now."

And so the merchant and one other adventurer joined the man in the orange caftan to float to the giant castle of the Perfect. Casting off, they heard the roar of a landslide and a mix of stifled yells and cries from where they had stood, and knew that the two who had stayed behind had ended their suffering.

The merchant and his fellow adventurer were shown to their quarters in the castle, in a beautiful hall of rooms filled with scores of the Perfect's servants. From them, the merchant learned about their host. It seems the castle was actually part of the quarry itself, built from suffering, beautified and enlarged whenever someone was made to suffer for the sake of perfection. The Perfect was a wizard who first discovered the castle and invented the dome of hot air to get there and supply it with necessities.

The Perfect appeared to be no more than thirty years old. The servants called the wizard "the Perfect" because it was everything anyone could ask for in human beauty—and when they beheld it, they could only want to look at it more, filling their blood with a warm excitement, feeding their hearts with energies and longing.

"I remember my family," one servant cried. "I was a mother of four. But now I want nothing more than to be near the Perfect! Even the wise-men and witches who come here have lost interest in their studies when they discover how very smart the Perfect already is."

In any case, the merchant was not worried, for over the months he had committed the sorcerer's spells to memory and could easily turn himself into a bird and fly away. But he was intrigued by the nature of the quest and decided to stay. He took to flying through the castle, inspecting everything. He believed that looking at the Perfect could do no harm if he remained a bird. However, when a person sees a beautiful orchid, or a wonderful horse, they can become entranced. To behold a gorgeous sunset can be captivating. To watch a rippling brook with the scent of water hyacinths is the same. And so it was for the bird, who took to sitting on the Perfect's window, becoming filled with song from morning to night.

After many weeks, the merchant became curious and wished to see the Perfect as a man would see it. He flew to the porch at the Perfect's window and changed to a man. The Perfect noticed the bird's song had stopped, and he came to the porch window.

"You would do well changing back to a bird, my good man, but I am afraid you won't want to see me again as a bird sees me. I should have to change you to a bird myself, for I enjoyed your singing."

Indeed, with the Perfect looking down at him as a man, the

merchant was filled with an incredible warmth and longing and understood everything the servants had spoken of. His greatest wish was to give the Perfect what it desired, to fulfill its every wish and whim. "Have mercy on me, Master," he addressed it. "Let me find you the Jewel of Perfect Justice. If I cannot, I will die for you!"

Thus it was that the merchant set out into the Quarry of Suffering. Walking over thousands of precious stones he quickly became bleary-eyed. Worse, with each step he could only think of the Perfect. *Oh my,* he thought. *What has become of me? I may not have the wits for this task anymore.*

When he picked up a giant ruby at his foot, he beheld a vision: children hidden in a church, set ablaze by their town's enemies, who slaughtered all who fled. In a garnet he saw a city tortured by the Plague. In an opal he beheld a crew of men huddled on a frozen boat; in a gold nugget he saw a leper colony and all its suffering. In the tiniest diamond he saw a crazed man pulling his hair and fingernails out. A ruby shimmered at his feet. He picked it up and in it were innocent convicts chained to their oars, being whipped under a blazing sun. He thought, *If this much made a ruby or a diamond, what would a simple crystal of salt show me?* He got down on his knees and dug through all the larger jewels to the soft crystals of sand below. He drew up a handful and looked deeply into one small crystal, and beheld a dog by his dead master. He looked at another, and saw a fawn standing by its lifeless mother.

The merchant cried out, "Ah, but I've found my spirit again!

"There's no suffering that can be paid for, nor can there ever be one single Jewel of Pure Justice to adorn the throne of the Perfect. The quest it has put to us is pure childishness!"

And in that instant he had a plan.

"In every quarry," he reasoned, "one comes upon seashells

that have lain at the bottom of forgotten seas. They too will remember suffering."

Turning himself into an eagle, he flew high over the quarry floor until he spied a giant conch. He flew down to it and became a man, who looked into it and saw fish flapping on a dried-up lake, with animals dying beyond, their tongues out.

"This will do well," the merchant mused. Flying back with the conch to the castle, he carved it into a beautiful cameo with an image of the Perfect on its face. When it was done, he sent it to the Perfect, saying he had found the Jewel of Perfect Justice.

The Perfect beheld the suffering in the cameo. It saw its own image, too, and understood. Indeed, when we look for justice ourselves, or try to fashion justice, it is only in our own image.

The Perfect sent for the merchant.

"You have answered my question nobly. Either way I should not have ended your suffering as you expected but would let you do as you wished."

And so each day after eating, the merchant became a bird, wishing only to sing on the Perfect's window.

**Flying back with the conch to the castle,
he carved it into a beautiful cameo.**

The Untying

Years went by, and the merchant grew much older, for this was not a magical land where everyone stays young.

The Perfect was now an old wizard. Its rooms had always been filled with faithful servants turned to cats and dogs, which it played with as it wished. With magic it turned its rooms into little worlds with fabulous games to play. But the merchant, singing on its window, saw that when the Perfect simply sat and fondled its pets, it contemplated the cameo on its throne. And when it looked into jewels from the quarry, it would cry.

One day the Perfect exclaimed, "So much suffering is caused by those obsessed with justice!"

Turning to the window, it called, "You, who sing to me all day—you, who fashioned the cameo of my throne—come down and give me a plan for the end of my days."

The merchant flew down from the window, again becoming the old man he was. "I have been thinking about the end of my days, too," he said, "as I sit singing odes to an image of human perfection."

"I'm hardly that anymore," said the Perfect.

"My memory does the singing," replied the merchant.

"My memory cries," said the Perfect. "I once had a twin sister who was deformed and sickly. As ugly as she was, she never lost faith in life up to her last childhood breath. I came to this castle seeking the meaning of that injustice. Since then I have taken a very wrong turn. I was created the perfect human specimen—a beautiful body with a powerful mind. Beauty and power is only for play. I created an army of playthings in the midst of the world's suffering. Everyone here plays and forgets what is around us—for what surrounds us is every sad story since the earth began."

The merchant was silent a long time. Then he said, "Each evening when I am a man in my room, I vow I will find a way to leave this place and become who I once was. I think of my mother—who died asking for her son. But in the morning I awake hungry again to see you and sing. Like Nature itself, I become hungry. Nature integrates and disintegrates us all as it tries to become the source of all things and all time. It grows and changes and churns in so many directions, and each part of Nature must struggle like its parent."

The Perfect looked at the cameo on its throne.

"You were very clever to create this cameo. I believe you can discover a strategy to free me, and yourself, and everyone else, of this place."

"Many years ago," the merchant continued, "I defeated a strange creature known as the Sphincter. Its riddle was that those who did not guess the truth would live on—while those who discovered the truth would never live to tell it. I thought I was the first to guess the truth and live—but I was no different than the rest. This life of perpetual hunger, play, and feasting is all that is left of me. My cleverness has turned to dung in my hands. My truths grow nothing in the earth.

"I once helped a sorcerer embrace death. I thought he was alone in thinking his own life's riddle was the greatest on earth. I was wrong. We all do. Each of us has two palms with fingers pointing in all directions at once, a paradox for each hand. One hand points to the people and things around us, the other points to our dreams—our memories, our fantasies, and our hopes.

These are our riddles. We spend our days trying to grab what is un-grabbable, when we could truly grasp this paradox. To be one with Nature is this paradox—it feels so very right. Yet Nature makes us hungry to disintegrate, reintegrate, and finally coincide on the one and only oneness of it all.

"Every night I remember, and each day I wish to play and forget. To be free of all thoughts that bind me. As a man, I let passing thoughts of this or that appear without announcing themselves, then disappear to make room for new memories. Such a collection of daydreams I am! To become a bird is to be one thing at a time. Yet a bird is thrown into many different places, one after another, and cannot find itself any better than a man. Better to be a worm."

The Perfect began pacing the room now. It seemed the merchant was getting nowhere.

"You are impatient," the merchant laughed, "but a strategy such as this must be woven one thread at a time. I can hardly see a pattern myself."

"Go on," smiled the Perfect. "We digest bread better when all the ingredients are mixed and baked."

And so the merchant went on: "This quarry must be the source of our strategy, for one way or another, we are all in its thrall. Claiming justice, men dig it wider with suffering. Even you have found that play and forgetfulness scrape at its walls.

"I was once a merchant. I created riches by searching for things that could be turned to value. I bought cheap and sold high. I see now that everyone values whatever riddle might free them of their own—becoming their own nature as they chase the riddle of Nature. Consider our hands as the riddles that bother us and move us along—and now look at the quarry. On one hand, it is filled with stones that people think valuable. On the other hand, each gem has been bought at the price of memories and lost dreams of people and time. This quarry represents men's riddles, and provides us our strategy.

"Seeing how you contemplated the cameo, I often went

back to the place it was found and pondered the gems around me. There are so many kinds of suffering, it is hard to comprehend. But the suffering was not about death, for with death one becomes Nature, integrated into the one and only whole. Rather the suffering was about the pain, the grief, and the fear—of wars within a mind, a body, a family, or a land—of truths being mocked and freedoms stolen. In small crystals I saw the suffering of trees and animals ripped for a time from their potential. In the end, all were relieved of their anguish to become one with all Nature. But it was not this they were truly born for.

"Each of these jewels speaks of hopes taken away before their time. You tried to forget suffering with games and play. Rather, we can embrace suffering as a doctor or religious person does—not to conquer death, but to lessen anguish wherever it is found, and to help others find their own nature in peace. These are truly the hands we've been given to play.

"The riddle of our fate is not answered through the lines on our palms, but through the lines on our fingers—spiraling inward from everyone around us, even from the fingers of those who have disintegrated in the mist of the past.

"We will become merchants—distributing jewels from this quarry. There is no true and perfect justice—for there can be no end to suffering in Nature itself. But all kinds of memories can be given life, to help create new lives and new futures. We will be connectors—merchants connecting the past to the future, and people to people. This is a different kind of justice, and the strategy I suggest will truly free us of this place."

And so this is what they did. Back and forth the floating dome traveled, carrying its occupants from the Perfect's castle to the land beyond the Quarry of Suffering. Each of the servants had been given jewels enough to start life over, and whether or not they believed what the Perfect explained about the gems, they soon became devoted to distributing a new kind of justice in the world. Released of the castle, released from their hunger, those who had emptied themselves of all thoughts soon found themselves with memories and dreams once again.

Having left the quarry, the old Im-Perfect, with the help of the old merchant, found craftsmen to create jewelry that spread the memories of the Quarry of Suffering. It was a strange jewelry that caused its owners to contemplate life anew, recognizing that the dreams of others could well be their own. To wear such jewels somehow released people from their own fears of suffering—a riddle if there ever was one—giving them a hearty appetite to do what they would to become what they could.

This ends the story of the merchant and his adventures, and while I suspect he had more, I haven't heard of them yet.

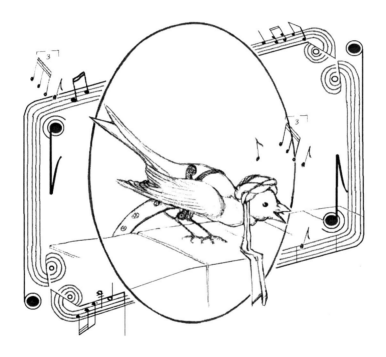

The Devil's Laugh

If someone introduces himself as the Devil and says, "You don't believe I'm *actually* Satan, but let's make a bet," don't shake on it. Whether he takes you by surprise, or you're skeptical, or curious as hell—don't put out your hand. You've got nothing to win. Besides that, you haven't proven a thing unless he *is* the devil, in which case you have everything to lose.

On the other hand, now that you can read my story, you can decide which suits you best—that is, whether to shake or not.

I was at this little film festival in Toronto for a friend of mine. I'm not a filmmaker, but my friend is. Sometimes I handle the camera, but mostly I dream up the gags and a lot of his visual set-ups. You can't believe how much of a film's interest depends on the visual and audio set-ups.

My friend's mom went into the hospital that week so I'd driven up to represent our film. It was first on the afternoon program, and there was a good-sized audience that gave me all my laughs at the right times. That got me pretty hyped, and when it finished I really wanted to celebrate with a drink. But I thought it looked rude to leave, so I hung out.

The next movie opened with a pan of a casino and sounds

of the slots. As the music cut in, they zoomed to this chick in hot-pants serving drinks and followed her to a blackjack table where a guy's eyes locked in on her. The music switched the moment he saw her, which tells us we're supposed to be inside his head and that he's the lead and it's *his* movie. That's about all I ever notice in a film …all the subliminal tricks. I can never remember the plot. Anyway, he buys his drink, pauses for a pick-up line, but thinks differently and turns back to the game. When he looks up for the deal, the camera switches to his "POV," or his point of view. We're the player now, and we see the dealer through his eyes: it's the devil dealing us our cards.

We know the dealer is Satan by the red glow in his pupils, like "red-eye" from an old flash camera. Otherwise, the guy isn't bright red or anything, he's just a character actor made up to look a bit devilish. They'd found a bald guy with a high skull and accentuated it with a little top-knot on his forehead. He had a great orange forked beard, and they'd elongated his ears and nose a bit. If you saw him on the D-train you'd figure he was a character actor on his way to play a crank or a caricature of a crazy uncle in an Off-Broadway show. So the red-eye effect, gleaming out of heavy eye-shadow, was just enough to do the trick.

But then they went over-the-top. The film switched to an overhead shot, and the cards the devil was dealing had a red-yellow glow to represent the smell of sulfur. Then, to make sure we "got it," all the players sniffed their cards and made a face when they picked up their hands. That was subliminal enough for me. I didn't wait for the plot, but got up and went down to the men's room.

When I was washing my hands, I looked up and recognized the guy next to me. It was the actor who played the devil. I did a double-take and said, "Hey, man. You're the devil!"

That's a pretty stupid line, but I was a bit creeped-out.

Then the guy answers "Yep!" and holds out his hand without

drying it, and adds, " I know you don't believe that I'm *actually* Satan, but I'll make you a bet ..."

I wasn't thinking. An actor sticks out his hand and you're at a film festival, so you shake it. I didn't realize I was taking the bet then and there. But as soon as I shook, the fellow laughed. He laughed the laugh of someone in control. It made me want to throw up. Can you imagine a laugh making you want to throw up?

I walk out on a guy's film and meet him in the men's room. Then I get sick to my stomach when I'm shaking his hand, and blame it on him. His laugh's disgusting, I think, but laughs don't make you throw up.

Well, just as I'm thinking that, another thought occurs to me, like, *I might have just lost a bet!* Because right then I felt pain run up my arms and down my back like a vibrating sunburn. I let go of his hand convulsively. He gurgled and cackled and shrieked with laughter. I felt my skin oozing. I could picture cellwalls breaking down, and I ran to a stall to retch. As I fell to my knees I heard him throw his head back with a laugh of conquest. He laughed on and on as I held tight to the throne. And his laugh kept changing. I never knew there were so many ways to laugh so evilly.

Gagging, I tried to remember that this wasn't my fault. I'd been wrong to shake, and was taking a ride for a mistake that anyone could have made. It had to end soon. I searched my brain for something to grab onto, to tell me what to do next. The classic shot from *Dr. Strangelove* flashed to mind: Slim Pickens riding the atom bomb to doomsday, waving his hat and hee-hawing like he was holding tight to a bronco. I chuckled and fell back into a nauseous swoon. Like I'd had my hand out on a merry-go-round—queasy and whipped around on my knees at a slow but dizzying speed—in that moment, I seem to have caught the ring.

"I think it's something in that laugh of yours that's making me sick," I coughed. He laughed harder. I looked up and did a double-take. Now he was sitting on the tank in front of me. He stepped on the silver button and his laugh merged merrily with the sound of flushing. I retched again, and as the pipes sucked my guts down the tube, he paused letting the sound of his laugh echo through the plumbing.

It was a great effect that it gave me just enough time to catch my breath. I held tight to the ring I'd caught just a moment before. It was my guess as to what was happening …a long shot.

"Your laugh has overtones no laugh can have. It isn't *you,* you know, it's those overtones! They're *not yours*!"

His laugh went hollow, if you could say that a stomach-turning nauseating cackle could go hollow.

"You can laugh yourself to death," I said.

There was a hiccup of a pause. It felt like I had only a few seconds left. I was frantic.

"That would be a good end for you. Just keep laughing!"

His face struggled with a thought. He couldn't answer me back. His infernal laugh stopped, the laugh that was my wild-card. So I played it.

"A laugh will kill you!

"A good laugh!

"A *real* laugh. A *belly* laugh."

What I was thinking, I don't know. It almost felt like I hadn't said it, though I'd heard the words clearly. So I reached up to touch my mouth and felt my teeth cave in. There was no tongue. Looking down, there were no fingers or hands, either. What was I feeling, phantom limbs? Fabulous. This was real great. I was gone. But I still had the power of speech.

"You've lost, you know. I'm still talking and you can't do anything more to me. My body is nearly gone, but as you notice, I'm the image of perfect calm after the storm."

His laughter had stopped, and I looked at him closely. Stripped of arrogance, he looked like a tired actor on the D-train.

"After all that, I landed my soul safely," I chuckled, "didn't I?"

There was silence. Like the quiet in a giant cathedral after the blasting chords of the organ. Then he mumbling something I couldn't catch, like, "You should take advantage of it while you have me down."

I no longer recognized him except for the orange beard and the topknot. He seemed dumber than I'd ever imagined.

"You actually don't understand things any more than an infant, do you? You weren't created as an adult. You're a cherub gone bad; nothing but an ancient, wicked child."

His shoulders were slumped and his eyes stared into space. I imagined he was looking at lost empires, desiccated civilizations sucked dry, his memories of the remains of millions of souls— all gone because of him.

My change to an angel or something had sobered the situation quite a bit. It was an intriguing twist that I'd kept my wits and escaped total destruction. I just needed to figure out where I stood. What could he do to me?

"They always say, 'knowledge is power,'" I smirked, "but I see that it is the other way around. Power is knowledge. It merely masquerades as knowledge, and tricks you into thinking it *is* knowledge. It tricked you, didn't it? But they're the same, and equally empty! Power isn't knowledge at all, is it?"

Caught up in pontificating, I hadn't noticed a change come over Old Nick. He was laughing again …rolling on the floor, laughing. He couldn't stop. He was giggling like a six-year old being tickled. He belly-laughed like he'd heard the oldest vaudeville joke with a fart for the punch-line. He couldn't control himself.

"Oh my God!," the devil blurted, "what ridiculousness!"

His laugh turned into Santa's at the department store.

"HO HO … Oh oh my God! HOHO HOoh my God!

"Oh HO HO HO oh Lord, thank you! It's wonnnnnnderful, HO you *are*! And *this* is SO very so silly! Thank you!"

What the devil was he talking about? How could *he* have said the word "God"?

He got up and skidded over the lavatory tiles, falling over again, in tears. "AAhhh. HO HO. It is so-oh funny to think of *this!* Oh, *thank* you for forgiveness! Thank you!"

His arms were splayed open and his eyes looked out, wet and warm and open. Then he caught his breath and pointed at me. "I can even love *you*," he said. He winked and started to giggle happily. Then he was quiet.

I'd like to say that he shriveled up and disappeared like the Wicked Witch of the West, but he didn't. His eyes opened wide and fixated on nothing, like he was dead. Meanwhile, the remains of what had been my body lay in the lavatory. Gore. I watched as a leg twitched. Not that I was worried about anybody finding us. Things like this seem to take care of themselves. They're cleaned up as soon as you walk away, like public toilets. They'd have to be, otherwise you'd read about more gruesome unsolved mysteries in the papers.

I won, I thought, *I really won.*

I had killed the devil with my wits intact. Disembodied and free! It was like I'd become an angel. I could still talk and think. It felt strong and convincing. Could I leave the room? Of course I could. I could go anywhere and be anywhere. In fact, I could be *everywhere!* I could see anything and become part of anyone. It was wonderful. It was destiny.

Did I ever tell you that since I was a kid I knew I was special? Now I knew I was *meant* to kill the devil. It had been my purpose in life.

But what did the devil think was *that* funny? I have no idea. And what had he mumbled? I don't know.

One thing I *do* know is that you think you understand my story. You think I've become the devil, and you're wrong. I've simply become a new angel or whatever. Someone will eventually come up with a name for me. Saint Frank the Miraculous or something. Frank used to be my name. And because it's no problem for me to insinuate myself onto the internet and generate text, I'll be able to come up with my own name and a mythology on Wikipedia to go with it. Like I just published this first eye-witness account of the devil being out-witted, by putting it on some guy's computer. He thinks *he* wrote it!

You are probably like I was. You convinced yourself when you were a kid that the devil never existed, or that evil's all relative. And the laughter bit? I mean it might have seemed evil at first, but laughter isn't evil by itself. Neither are those overtones evil. They're just relative. Let me explain it to you, the way I see it. I've figured out how to produce those overtones—the ones that made me nauseous. The overtones come with a special class of laughter called the "laugh of wisdom," and it works with a category of setups. Setups in life work just like in film, with events that call for resolution. That's all a laugh points to, or represents. That's all any emotion points to—the relationships built into sensory events. The chemistry of events and the chemistry of the body work together that way.

You put a thought in someone's mind and it has to be unfolded. Give someone a thought and they will seek resolution, and follow that thought like puppets. Just like in the movies. People act out the most bewildering fantasies. Each thought becomes a string. And this is how you set up a laugh of wisdom. Each string becomes a dozen associations that gets tied to your puppet. They can't break free of them, and it's the relationships between the thoughts that do all the work, not me. I just provide the setups, and let them tie themselves up. It's hilariously rich to watch the drama play out.

At first, everyone thinks the world is relative to them. Suddenly it's not, and it's this moment of recognition that's your pay-off. You watch them convulse, their eyes widening with agony, believing some evil has taken over. It's not evil, but wickedly funny. The joke is that they're going to find out it makes no difference in the end. It's about here that the laugh takes off. It's the sound that does the work, of course. No other sound is like it. To laugh that laugh is the most wonderful feeling in the universe. It has something extra, something indescribable about it—which are the overtones, of course. Once that laugh gets reverberating, it unfolds with harmonics that no one can conceive of. I suspect they're harmonics that physical bodies can't participate in, only incorporeal bodies like mine can feel it. It's the overtones of that laugh that pulled me apart to become this kind of super-angel. It's kind of complicated, so I don't expect you to understand. But it was my incredible insight about knowledge and power that made the devil laugh again. He'd been confused and he suddenly saw the irony. When he realized how incredibly simple it all becomes in the end, the last laugh was on him.

MUMENALI AND THE ONIONS

or,

The Old and Original Tale of Why Onions Make Us Cry

Mumenali and the Sufi's Task

Very long ago, in Turkistan, even before Timur the Terrible built Samarkand, there was a powerful and wicked king named Mumenali the Bulgar. He was getting old and stout and had no heirs to give his kingdom to when he died. What he feared most was that one day soon his guards and visitors would abandon him in his old age and support any young rival that should come along. So Mumenali was very jealous of the many young and strong princes that dwelled in neighboring territories, especially his closest neighbor, Altan Beterbeg, who was not only young and strong, but also well-loved, and whose reputation for goodness grew greater each year. Mumenali thought seriously that if he didn't destroy Altan Beterbeg, his own guards would suggest to his viziers, and his viziers would suggest to his ministers, to lock old Mumenali up in the tower dungeon and offer the good and charitable Altan Beterbeg the throne.

So now, although Altan Beterbeg had never done him any harm, old Mumenali thought of him as a most terrible enemy, and spent his days scheming of how to destroy this good neighbor.

It so happens, however, that Mumenali the Bulgar was not really a stupid man. He had been clever enough to become as powerful as he was, and he knew he could easily destroy Altan

Beterbeg's army, and with it, the young pasha's reputation. Holding onto power is not as easy as getting it in the first place and then holding onto life. Mumenali knew he was already an old man, and this made him worry that all his plans might not be worth it. Wars always tired him out, and intrigues made Mumenali nervous that something would go wrong and backfire. Mumenali began wondering how many years he would have to savor the accomplishment of destroying his young neighbor. A new and costly war might not be worth it if he had only a few years to live. So Mumenali the Bulgar had the most famous advisor in all of Asia summoned to his palace, to ask him what course to take.

The wise man's name was WatWat, and he was made famous by having been the chief counselor to Harun al-Rashid (whom you can find in history books and in the tales of the Arabian Nights and in the tales of Sinbad the Sailor). However, Mumenali made a mistake in calling for WatWat—for the wise man was a Sufi, and Sufis are religious men. Thus it was that although WatWat was paid to give counsel to kings, he hated wars and intrigues of any kind. He was a clever man who had made kingdoms strong by organizing their trade and building water systems. People said he was the wisest man in the world, and after many years passed, WatWat began to believe it, too. But WatWat was most famous as a seer, a person who reads people's futures in the stars and who tells fortunes. One month after Mumenali the Bulgar summoned him, WatWat arrived with all his equipment (thirty mules were just enough to carry it all).

WatWat climbed down off his smiling old camel with some difficulty. He had as a young man been quite thin and would nimbly glide down holding his stirrup straps, but as it is said, "he put success under his belt" (which means he had gotten quite stout), and now needed page-boys to bring his gold and sky-blue camel-ladder in order to dismount. This all made quite a spectacle, and of course his hosts were always impressed, as WatWat's camel had never learned to kneel.

So it was that WatWat entered Mumenali's courtyard, dismounted, and strutted up to the waiting king, never once bowing his head. WatWat considered himself to be one of the greatest philosophers of the world and was quite sure that this Mumenali the Bulgar could not have any problem out of the ordinary. When Mumenali ushered the Sufi into the throne room, and confidentially explained the trivial designs for destroying his neighbor, asking the Sufi in all seriousness if it was worth it, and whether he would live long enough to enjoy a victory, WatWat only laughed silently to himself. He was used to dealing with cutthroats and brigands, and particularly with petty tyrants like Mumenali the Bulgar.

I will teach this little king a thing or two, and get paid for it into the bargain. These shallow fellows are always more impressed with the equipment than with my good sense. Let's just see what we can concoct, the Sufi thought. So WatWat had all his thirty mules unloaded out onto the palace floor, and spread before Mumenali the most magnificent array of horoscopal and crystal-gazing devices that could be seen anywhere in that time or this. Needless to say, Mumenali was exceedingly impressed. In fact, WatWat's fortune-telling equipment left the king speechless.

WatWat bowed low to his host and began muttering some mystical-sounding words. Mumenali watched as the tubby wise man huffed and puffed from one piece of machinery to another, setting all the paraphernalia in motion. WatWat would turn his crystals this way and that, look deeply at them for a moment, mutter something, and wander off as if he were in a trance. Looking as if he were stumbling on a box, into it his hand would suddenly shoot and throw a handful of sulfurous dust into the air. Calmly he would watch it fall, but then he would be off, only to begin something else just as bizarre and wonderful. For nearly an hour the portly Sufi ran helter-skelter and made quite a show, looking at candle drippings, throwing sticks, and swirling tea leaves from China. Finally he stopped and wiped the perspiration from his brow with a big green bandana.

WatWat bowed low to the king.

"You wanted me to tell you if you would live long enough to enjoy the destruction of your neighbor's kingdom?"

"That is correct," Mumenali answered, on the edge of his throne.

"Please, Sire." WatWat held his bandana to his forehead. "You must spare me the pain of telling you!"

Mumenali bolted upright.

"What have the stars foretold?" he blurted out. "What have your candles and crystals and sulfur and stars all foretold for me? Am I to die? Surely not! Speak, Sufi. I have paid you to tell me!"

You can be sure it was Mumenali who was perspiring now. His veins stood out like copper wires on his forehead. He was scared stiff after the Sufi's performance.

WatWat remained calm. He bowed low again.

"Sire, I am honored you have brought me here to give you my wise counsel. But Sire, it is worse than even you have just now guessed. For the wax from the candles of Persia, the crystal balls of India and Baghdad, the sulfur from the deepest mines of the earth, and the stars in the sky have all given the same exact reply.

" 'What man's future are you asking?' they all say. 'This Mumenali the Bulgar, King of Turkistan, has been dead already many years.'"

WatWat paused to give the best effect possible and then continued. "I thought there must have been a mistake, so I set the same question to them all over again, repeating all of my trouble a second time. The second reply was even quicker than the first.

"'Dead already—no fortune!'"

Mumenali was so surprised his jaw dropped open, and it

dropped so wide in fact, as it is said, "on his teeth a camel could find a nice seat" (which means to say, *very* wide).

He stood up trembling, astounded by this news, and felt his way over to the royal mirror, for he was half afraid he could no longer walk, and he was really afraid that he wouldn't see his own reflection in the mirror.

WatWat was enjoying himself immensely, but to look at him he seemed very serious and concerned for the welfare of the monarch.

"Wh-*why* do the fortunes answer m-me like this?" stammered the frightened king.

"C-can there be a mistake, for I seem to be as well and in one piece as I've ever been?" Mumenali's eyes looked wild, and he began flailing his arms about as he wandered all over the throne room.

"Why, I haven't seen a cemetery in years, let alone been seen lying in one," the flustered king continued. "Or am I just a ghost and merely dreaming in my deathly slumber? And if I'm dead, who could this WatWat fellow be that is visiting me in heaven?"

WatWat giggled softly but was eloquent.

"Sire, calm yourself. Your body is most surely here, for I myself am quite alive, and can see you and can certainly hear you. But you have misunderstood. When the fortunes speak, it is only with regard to a person's spirit, and apparently your own has been dead quite some time."

Mumenali looked up at him quizzically.

WatWat went on. "You are known as a wicked king, isn't that true?"

Mumenali relaxed quite a bit and smiled rather proudly. "Yes, you might say I am the most thoroughly disliked king in all this part of the world. I doubt you could find my equal anywhere for thinking up evil and pernicious taxes and for executing ministers for no other reason than to put fear and obedience into the hearts of my subjects. I also do quite a good job at having my men plunder merchants on the highway, if I think they have charged me too much on their last visit. I am quite good at taking my revenges with an innocent-looking smile."

Mumenali demonstrated a sweet smile for the Sufi.

WatWat smiled back.

"Well, Sire Mumenali the Bulgar, your wickedness has not increased your favor with the fortunes. I imagine I could not find your equal in these parts for being thoroughly unhappy and downright empty-in-the-soul, either, now could I?"

Mumenali's face went sour at these words.

"Your Most High-ness," WatWat continued. "What my fortune-telling devices have said for you must be true. Your heart is empty and your spirit has slowly decayed away. No one in this world cares that you live; in fact they all wish that you were dead."

Mumenali was beginning to feel ashamed in front of this plump but thoroughly wise philosopher. But WatWat was not yet through.

"You have asked me here to find out if you would live long enough to *enjoy* the destruction of Altan Beterbeg and his kingdom. Doesn't that seem very silly indeed?"

The old tyrant suddenly looked very tired. He looked around at all the Sufi's learned equipment, strewn here and there across the palace floor, the candles still smoking, a smell of sulfur still in the air, and crystal balls reflecting their incandescent gloom from the unknown. Mumenali got down on his knees in front of the wise man.

"Is there no way that I can become alive again?" he pleaded.

WatWat's plan had worked better than he had ever expected. He thought for a moment seeking a sufficient reply to give this silly king. Suddenly he had it.

"I have already insisted upon such advice from the fortunes

themselves," WatWat said. "They said you must become a changed man."

Mumenali looked up at him imploringly. "But how will such a thing be possible? I am already such an old man!"

WatWat looked at him chidingly, as if he had no right to question the fortunes' wisdom, and replied only, "The task they have chosen for you, to make your spirit live, is to change yourself so that even your worst enemy, this Altan Beterbeg, would cry tears should misfortune befall you."

So saying, WatWat bowed low and began to gather up his equipment.

Mumenali sat on the throne room floor, dumbfounded, as the Sufi packed. Finally the king stood up and thanked WatWat with all the words he knew how, and as the wise man's thirty mules were loaded up, the king ordered that forty camels laden with silk and precious saffron be prepared to pay the famous Sufi.

Thus it was that WatWat went away richer and feeling wiser than ever before. Yet Mumenali was disconsolate, for as the Sufi had ascended his gold and sky-blue camel-ladder, head held high and proud, Mumenali the Bulgar, king of all Turkistan had turned away—and with his head bowed low, shuffled into the palace garden to think deeply.

All he could hear were those parting words, "To become alive you must change yourself so that even Altan Beterbeg would cry tears should misfortune befall you." No one could have looked more contrite and desolate than did Mumenali, then and there in his garden.

He was about to become converted to WatWat's way of thinking.

No doubt he understood the Sufi's reasoning, and his interpretation of the fortunes' reply. Mumenali knew well enough that inside himself he was truly dead, and that he no longer enjoyed or appreciated the smallest morsel of his achievements. He had not a bit of spirit left alive in him.

But how was he to change? Neither the fortunes nor the wise man had given him the slightest clue. Turning the Sufi's words this way and that, imagining every conceivable interpretation, and looking for every possible nuance of meaning, Mumenali stumbled on his only chance of success.

Like many a new convert, he decided to take WatWat's words quite literally.

"I must change? Why, *that* cannot present such a difficult problem. Men change every day from one thing to another. From bad to worse, from camel-driver to mule-driver, from young man to old man. At the marketplace only last week I saw a clever fakir change himself into a cat! The fortunes themselves said nothing about my becoming *good*. Gracious, *that* possibility is well nigh impossible for an old villain like me.

"Sufi WatWat is certainly *so* wise that he didn't think it worth mentioning that the fortunes cannot be bargained with. A man cannot take back his wicked deeds once they are done. As it is said, 'Just a word, once spoken, is like an arrow already shot—it cannot be taken back.'

"Even for all the harm a vicious word can cause, how much more terrible are the real arrows I have had my army and guards shoot for me. What I have destroyed I cannot replace, and I have been so wonderfully, awfully wicked! I have left children without homes and farmers without fields (I won't worry about the merchants I've ruined; they asked for it).

"Sufi WatWat is much too wise, and becoming 'good' cannot be what the fortunes have set to be my task.

"Surely I must change into some animal or another that Altan Beterbeg pities. In stories when the fortunes set tasks for the heroes, they must solve these by cleverness and guile."

The little king went on like this for several hours, wandering aimlessly, then stomping vigorously about his palace garden. Still, he couldn't arrive at a plan for changing himself in order to gain back his life.

Dead already … no fortune.

Mumenali the Bulgar Gains Back Life

Mumenali was walking to and fro like this in his garden, so worried over his problem that he didn't notice he had walked right into a clump of ragweed. Now, hay fever is just as old as any other nuisance, and the king was just as allergic as you or I (and especially grown-ups tend to be today). Suddenly he let out an awful sneeze.

Another sneeze. And another, and another! No one was there to say "God bless you," and no one would have cared to say it anyway to old Mumenali, people hated him that much. But somewhere in the world, at that exact moment, someone must have said, "God bless you," because in all his sneezing, Mumenali hit upon his idea.

Mumenali the Bulgar hastened to his courtroom and called all his ministers and viziers together. One after another he gave them jobs to do and proclamations to send out. He had the killing of cats forbidden throughout the land and sent one minister out to search for the fakir he had seen in the marketplace. He had another set to supervise the claiming of every seventh chicken from the farmers as a "holiday tax." He made things even more insufferable for his people, and the king of Turkistan didn't look about to change his ways very quickly.

Then he sent a minister to have packages of every species of weed or vegetable, flower or fruit collected from every man with a garden who lived within a hundred miles of the palace. And he sent a vizier to order all the walls in his kingdom over three feet wide be measured and marked with a big green check. Besides this, he prohibited the boiling of fat after 6 PM, the wearing of yellow in public places, and he ordered that bells be put on the sandals of every man or woman over fifty years old.

If anyone shirked his new edicts it was well understood that they would be imprisoned. In short, Mumenali had made up a whole list of proclamations that made him look more wicked than ever, and all these new orders were without rhyme or reason, a state of affairs that aggravated all the people of his realm even more.

"It would be understandable if old Mumenali demanded money for the treasury," his viziers grumbled, "but *every seventh chicken* for a 'holiday tax?'

"What are we going to do with all these chickens?"

"It would be understandable," said the landowners, "if the king said he needed stones for a new palace—we would find him the stones without taking apart our nice, thick walls. Why must he have them all measured and marked with this horrible ugly green check?"

The old people were equally furious: "If our wicked old king wants to round us all up and put us to work he should spend his money on giving us crutches. But *bells?* What humiliation! Our grandchildren laugh at us, and the village tea-house sounds like a flock of sheep have arrived to play Parcheesi."

"Oh, the ignominy of it all!" cried the citizens.

"What is Mumenali the Bulgar up to?" was the question on everyone's mind.

"I am afraid to ask," was the answer heard on everyone's lips.

The fakir was found on the very first day, and now packages

had begun to arrive with samples of fruits, vegetables, and weeds from throughout the kingdom. A fakir is another name for a magician, but mostly for the "holy men" in Persia and India and Turkistan who made their living by performing stunts such as lying on beds of nails, swallowing flaming torches, and, in this instance, turning into household animals.

Mumenali kept himself extremely busy studying with the fakir, and going through all of the packages that his ministers were bringing him daily. Several weeks passed and Mumenali's mood became markedly changed. He now hustled around the palace humming little ditties to himself. He frequently chuckled, and it was even rumored that he clicked his heels secretly under his royal robes while sitting on his throne attending to affairs of state.

One day he passed a law ordering flower-boxes to be built onto all the walls that were now marked with green checks. When this was done he had a funny green grass planted in each and every one of them. He had his royal artists paint signs to be posted throughout his realm. But the signs were full of nonsense rhymes, and nobody could understand a word of them.

The viziers and ministers got angrier and angrier. They had never been made to work so hard. And all for what? Only Mumenali the Bulgar seemed to know, and he just worked harder and harder, sweating and chuckling to himself.

He had turned out to be a very good student. After only two months of studies with the fakir, the little tyrant, Mumenali, could change himself into a rooster and a frog. Several lessons later he had mastered the art of turning into a palace goldfish, and after some very hard work he had learned the hardest trick of all—to turn into a delicate tulip. He was very pleased with himself and paid the fakir handsomely, only, of course, after vowing him to secrecy. No one must know what Mumenali was up to, otherwise how could he hope to trick the fortunes?

With the fakir gone, Mumenali decided that now all was ready. He only needed the finishing touches to put his plan into action, and he was full of expectation. Old Mumenali didn't know when he had ever had so much fun.

He called his ministers and viziers before him. Reluctantly they came, expecting more evil and senseless decrees, and even more work to enforce them. Mumenali sat straight and proud in his throne. He thumped his fist impatiently as they walked in to let them know he was still Mumenali the Wicked. He was enjoying himself immensely as he watched each of their forlorn faces file before him, for nothing could please him more than to watch their faces drop still lower. Oh, how he hoped he wouldn't disappoint them.

For his newest proclamation was this: Mumenali forbade anyone to throw olive or date pits onto the street.

Anyone—including his guards, ministers, children, or dogs—caught violating this decree was to be arrested on the spot and carted off to jail.

Now this may seem very petty to you or me, but it was a highly inconvenient law for the people of Mumenali's realm. They were accustomed to constantly pop dates or olives into their mouths as they walked from place to place—rather as you or I would eat candy. But because no one had pockets built into their clothes (where we would stuff the candy wrappers), Mumenali's edict meant that everyone would have to leave the date and olive pits stuffed in their cheeks (which would make talking rather difficult), or they would have to quit eating olives and dates while they walked.

The ministers and viziers imagined everyone talking with mouths full of olive and date pits, and their faces fell to never-before-reached depths of woe. Mumenali was satisfied.

As soon as they were outside the palace, the ministers and viziers exploded with rage. As it is said, "There is always one last straw which will break the camel's back," which is to say that this last small demand met with open revolt. The ministers talked it over with the viziers, and the viziers told the guards.

They sent a secret delegation to Altan Beterbeg, asking him to support them in a war against Mumenali.

The young pasha, however, always having the most honorable intentions, insisted that he would support a revolt only on the conditions that the wicked tyrant should refuse to take back his whole list of new and senseless decrees. And when he said this, in fact, Altan Beterbeg proposed that he himself should go before Mumenali and make this demand.

The young king knew that only he could safely appear before Mumenali and make such a demand, for any of Mumenali's ministers to do so would be quickly executed for treason. So the ministers agreed to let the young pasha make the trip to Mumenali's palace, to appear personally before him with his ultimatum. And if Mumenali refused, then they would go to war.

Altan Beterbeg traveled with all haste, accompanied personally by an escort of Mumenali's own palace guards. Soon he found himself trumpeted and announced at the palace gates, and contrary to what everyone expected, he was joyfully greeted by an already waiting king, and ushered privately into the throne room.

Mumenali did not even scream or stamp his feet.

Amazing, thought his viziers. We had better be on our guard, for he is surely up to something.

And that he was. Altan Beterbeg explained his ultimatum— that either Mumenali take back all of his latest decrees or the young pasha would use his own army to support a palace revolt.

"My good young neighbor," replied Mumenali, smiling sweetly to show all of his thirty-two gold teeth, "you know that even if my own palace guards rise up against me, I need only open the treasury to hire a whole new crew. For such pay as I'll offer I can find a very bloodthirsty army to fight you.

"There would be battles and broken skulls. And you know that wars always tire me out." Mumenali sighed compassionately.

"My good friend Beterbeg!" The little tyrant's eyes lit up as he continued. "Instead of all this trouble you're proposing on my behalf, what would you say to a duel between you and me?"

The younger man was startled. Mumenali the Bulgar was old and fat. He was probably even too weak to lift a sword, whereas Altan Beterbeg was one of the greatest swordsmen in all of Asia, and had never turned down the chance for a duel in his life. Everyone knew he always won.

This seemed a very strange affair to the young pasha Beterbeg, who had come to Mumenali's palace full of fears and apprehensions. All of his fears seemed to have vanished. He had been cordially welcomed, and hadn't even aroused the older king's anger at the mention of a palace revolt. Of course, what he said about hiring an army was true, and apparently old Mumenali hadn't the slightest intention of taking back his decrees. So Altan Beterbeg accepted the proposal of a duel without hesitating, if only to save the lives that would be lost in battle.

So the arrangements for the combat were made. A large field outside the city walls was fixed with bleachers for the spectators and with tents to serve food. Flags were strung up with the colors of both kingdoms displayed everywhere. The preparations went on for weeks. All the while the ministers conjectured, the guards and viziers took bets, and the people talked excitedly. In the meantime, the funny green grasses grew taller in the flowerboxes on all the walls over three feet wide.

The day of the duel arrived. As the sun rose higher, the day grew scorching hot. At noon the trumpeters sounded the hour of the duel.

The two kings faced each other at opposite ends of the field. Altan Beterbeg was tall and fearsome. His large black mustache was braided and knotted into two clubs and his oiled muscles glistened in the white-hot sun. He sneered the sneer of a warrior.

Mumenali's eyes gleamed, but that's about all that looked fresh and young. He had certainly grown pudgy after so many years of just sitting on his throne. In fact, now that he was off of his high throne, everyone in his realm saw surprisingly that their king, Mumenali the Wicked, was no taller than a hunched-over water carrier. The people were jubilant. Mumenali was sure to lose, and that would be an end to all their troubles. Even should he win, he had agreed to let Altan Beterbeg's son rule in peace—and not only that, but had agreed to make Beterbeg's son his own eventual heir. And he did this all for the sake of his silly decrees.

But of course we know he did it all for the sake of Sufi WatWat, and the task the fortunes had decided on "to gain back life."

Now, perhaps you've already guessed that the funny grasses Mumenali had planted in the flower-boxes were onions. Just before the day of the duel, the little king had them all pulled up and prepared to be served at the food tents at the duel site. Thousand of them. He had them stewed, he had them fried with potatoes—just like your home fries—and he even had the biggest ones stuffed with meatloaf and baked. Nobody had ever seen or tasted onions before, and in those days they didn't yet make people cry. And the signs he had his royal artists paint that nobody could understand? Well, they were all about onions. Here are some examples:

"Eat onions, good for bunions!"

"Here's the news: best in stews."

"From a pot or a pan, if you can't give it flavor, add an onion, it can!"

You see, when Mumenali was in the garden thinking, and the ragweed made him sneeze, he'd had an idea.

If one plant makes people sneeze, another must make people cry, he thought. So he had his ministers bring him those packages of plants from all over his kingdom. He would secretly find the one that made people cry. But he had little luck. The royal assembly room looked more like a farmer's market. In just one little corner there was cauliflower, collard, cattails, bladderwort, gooseberries, goats-beard, persimmon, kale, rutabagas, snapdragons, Barbary figs, anise, mustard, and jute! But nothing would make Mumenali cry a single tear.

"Nothing works! Nothing makes me cry!" Mumenali finally screamed in fury and despair at the plants. "Do you hear me, you wretched weeds? You must make men cry, just once if I am to win my life back, and I will do anything for you, *anything!*"

The poor king was stamping and kicking and throwing a tantrum by this time, when, to his surprise, a little onion at his feet timidly answered back.

"We can certainly do as you wish if you will only make us onions better known. We are a very talented vegetable, and will certainly make men cry—but alas, we go unused. What are soups and salads without us? How can a stew survive? But no, we are a wretched and sad vegetable, left to live our whole lives unknown."

Old Mumenali was happy beyond all expectation, and from then on his spirits brightened.

"I'll have my ministers plant you throughout the kingdom, and I'll have my poets write your praises. I shall even have you grown to be fit for a sultan's table and will serve you in a banquet to all my people! Can you really make men cry?"

The onion was quick to respond, "Just cut a little piece from my bulb and pass it under your nose, and behold, I'll bring tears to your eyes."

And it all happened just as the onion said it would. Mumenali cried. But soon he was crying tears of joy, for he could succeed in his plan for outwitting the fortunes and performing their impossible task: "that Mumenali must change himself so that even his enemy Altan Beterbeg would cry tears should misfortune befall him."

Yes, now Mumenali was surer than ever.

But of course the fortunes weren't being outwitted at all,

for it was very clear that new life had entered the spirit of Mumenali the Bulgar already, for the little tyrant was very lovingly preparing a *most* elaborate joke.

Of course we already know that he kept his promises to the onion. He even had the largest and most beautiful onion prepared and sent by special courier to the table of the great Sultan Harun al-Rashid (Sufi WatWat's famous employer), but this is beside the point. The day of the great duel has already been described, and if we try hard, we will remember the silly decrees, the studying with the fakir, and the enraging of his ministers who wanted to revolt. All of this Mumenali had very carefully planned to lead up to this special day.

The drums began to roll, and the two kings silently approached the center of the great arena. It wasn't really all that silent. Mumenali the Bulgar could hardly walk under all his leather and gold and shining copper armor. He sounded like a pot and kettle salesman coming into town and clanging his wares. Altan Beterbeg, sleek as a leopard, and wearing no armor at all, got to the center long before Mumenali, and waited, snickering at his opponent's approach.

As soon as poor Mumenali got within a stone's throw of the young warrior, he raised his sword above his head and let out a little yelp. Beterbeg looked, and Mumenali was running toward him, waving his sword with great difficulty above him, and shouting a very funny-sounding war cry at the top of his voice. Quite amused, Altan Beterbeg stepped aside. Poor Mumenali ran right past and Beterbeg let out a merry laugh. Mumenali stopped and turned around. He was huffing and puffing and could hardly lift his blade for another try. Actually, he could hardly have cared less, for he was only concentrating on the task the fortunes had set for him. He summoned some strength in his old, flabby arms to swing at the young pasha several more times. *After all, this has to look like a duel,* he thought.

Altan Beterbeg was leaning on his giant curved scimitar, just laughing and laughing. Soon the whole crowd joined in.

Is this short and fat man really the wicked Mumenali Bulgar who made all of Turkistan shudder under his awful reign? Altan Beterbeg thought angrily. *This duel is making a mockery of me! This tyrant has done the last wickedness of his life. I will finish him off in one blow and be done with both him and this joke of a duel!*

Mumenali had been waiting for the young warrior to lose his patience. The young pasha raised his blade above his head for one mighty blow, and as Mumenali approached for yet another futile swing, Beterbeg's blade whistled down on the little king.

Altan Beterbeg felt his sharp scimitar cut Mumenali in two, from his head to his toes. The crowd let out a cheer! "The wicked tyrant is dead!" they all cried. But then suddenly, the cheering stopped. As if it was one giant person, the stadium uttered a single gasp, then there was a babble and yelling that sounded like a stampeding heard of trumpeting elephants.

Altan Beterbeg looked around for the cause of all this commotion, but—of all the strange things!—he couldn't see anything through all the tears in his eyes! Altan Beterbeg Pasha, a grown man, was crying harder than a little boy. Now he was sure he had killed the wicked little king, but he couldn't see him anywhere. When he wiped away the tears, things were not better at all. For what he beheld before him, inside all of Mumenali the Bulgar's fancy armor, were the two severed halves of a giant onion, lying at his feet.

The crowd was amazed. Where was Mumenali? Nobody in the stadium knew. Nobody but Sufi WatWat. He had heard about the duel and had secretly come to watch. At first he only giggled to himself that Mumenali could have been so foolish. But soon he stopped laughing, for he saw that what Mumenali had done was courageous indeed. He knew he could not change his ways so quickly or easily as Sufi WatWat had made it sound. Mumenali had fought for life the only way he knew how, with stratagems and guile, and he sacrificed even himself for the sake of giving his spirit back life. So the Sufi left the stadium feeling much less wise than he had upon entering. Not only that, he sold his camel with the gold and sky-blue camel-ladder to another stout, rich man. And Sufi WatWat walked out of town alongside his pages and his thirty mules. He also vowed he would not play jokes on anyone with his learned equipment anymore.

When there is enough free food to feed two armies and all the people of a city, you can bet that people will have a feast. In fact, they loved the onions Mumenali had prepared. And it wasn't long before they understood the meaning of all the silly-sounding signs their late king had put throughout his kingdom, which was now Altan Beterbeg's kingdom.

And Altan Beterbeg proved to be a wise and just ruler. But almost everyone came to agree that Mumenali the Bulgar had always been an onion in disguise; in fact, myths and stories began to be told that he was none other than an onion king, and some said he was the ruler of all the vegetables. But of course that's just how stupid tales get started, and exaggerated out of all proportion. One thing is for sure, onions have made men cry ever since, in commemoration of the little king's courage.

The Evil Eye and the Rosebush

There is a little town on the Mediterranean in Southern France with a harbor full of fishing boats. It was a port before the Phoenicians ever arrived, and was probably known in the days of Odysseus because of the perfect little harbor behind a giant and dramatic red rock called "the Eagle's Beak," which sailors could see from far off. Fishing boats still sit in the giant rock's shadow, along with a forest of giant cranes from the days when they built supertankers there. The town is called La Ciotat, which means "the city" in an old Mediterranean dialect.

But this is not a tale about seafarers, it is a tale about a rosebush. It could be a very ancient story as old as the town, but it happened in the days when they built the big supertankers there. That's when I lived in La Ciotat.

Before I tell the story, however, I must tell you how it got into this book, for that itself deserves a short preface. As I've said, it's the story of a rosebush. But it is also the story of the evil eye. I think it was because of the evil eye that I was never able to get a picture of the rose or transcribe the story from my notebook for nearly thirty years. For when I went to type the handwritten version, as in the story itself, something would happen to stop me. My keyboard would unaccountably lock up or my computer would crash. But it only happened when I went to type *this* story, mind you, none of my others.

Not long ago something came up that got me thinking about the story again. I finally figured it out, and decided to sit down and try typing it once more. This time it worked. I got the story down, with a new ending. Now, there was this old rosebush in my backyard that hadn't bloomed all summer; but just before the first frost of winter, a single white and peach flower finally appeared, and as it wilted another bud grew right out of the center of the first. And so I figured I got the story right this time, and here it is.

I am an artist. Every day while we lived in La Ciotat, my wife and I walked through town to find a new place to sit, where she would read and I would paint. In the evenings, in the cafes along the port, we sold paintings from previous days. After that, I would work late into the night to complete the day's paintings, cut mats, and make frames for the ones I'd try selling tomorrow. I also did the cooking, but my wife did the laundry by hand and wrote letters home.

If I wasn't painting the harbor, we would walk above town to find gardens and houses and views of the sea, in places where my wife could find a shady place to sit and read. While I would sit in the hot sun and paint. As long as the paintings are selling, what a life to be the artist's wife!

The road to the hills above town ran along the cemetery wall. At the bottom of the hill were shops that sold ornaments and enamel bouquets. The first of these, at the corner of the alley alongside the Post Office, was a small cottage with a giant gnarly rosebush growing up its wall and over its roof.

The sidewalk ran right under that bush, but cars were usually coming by, so we stuck to the sidewalk and ducked carefully to avoid its sharp grey thorns. Looking up one day I noticed the rose. Not fully open, it was white, then cream, and at the tips of its petals, peach.

Several days later I looked to see it in full bloom, but it

wasn't there. Instead, a little to the right and a bit higher up was another perfect rose, exactly like the first.

The third time this happened I was very surprised. So we decided to pass the cottage the next day, and the next, and sure enough, there was never more than one rose on the bush. Always new, always perfect, and never, ever, in full bloom.

The bush was so big and the cottage so tiny, it looked right out of a fairy tale. I had to paint a picture of it—perhaps for a story about a rosebush that always grew one perfect rose. But the street was much too busy and narrow and it offered no place to sit. So I decided to take a photograph, which even famous painters do sometimes.

The next day I got there early to take my photo, for the dew in the air gives a wonderful glow to the morning, and the light on your subjects seems to come from everywhere. As I was framing my shot, a lady coming from market rushed up out of breath.

"Monsieur! Monsieur! Don't shoot the picture!"

She looked me in the eye and touched her eye, then made the sign of the cross. For this is what they do around the Mediterranean Sea so as not to speak of the "Evil Eye." Then she whispered hoarsely:

"*She* is at the window looking right at you! The papers just wrote that burglars from Marseilles are posing as photographers."

"But I am just taking a picture of her beautiful rose," I explained.

"Monsieur, photograph *anything* in this town but not her rosebush! Haven't you heard its story?" The market lady took hold of my sleeve and pulled me up the street.

"We call her 'the Rose Widow,' for many years ago her husband brought her this rosebush as a gift. As he was planting it, someone came to tell them their son had been killed in an accident at the shipyards.

"When the first rose bloomed, her husband had a heart

attack. Every day since then the bush has given her a bloom for the family's grave, for that bush has taken both her son and her husband."

The lady from the market made the sign of the cross and walked quickly up the street.

"She is still watching," she called back. "Leave, quickly!"

I thought of the "eternal rose" that grew from the hero's graves in fairy tales and folk songs. Here it was in real life! A single perfect rose that was always on that gnarly old bush. Faith overcoming the tragedy for this simple lady selling markers for the graves of others.

I ran home to tell my wife. Of course I didn't believe in the evil eye, but just *had* to have a picture. And so, later that afternoon. we approached the widow's house from behind the concrete power poles along a dusty alley at the bottom wall of the cemetery. These poles have holes or "windows" cut through them to make them lighter, and so I set my camera on the open shelf in one of them and carefully leaned over to adjust the shot.

"She's in the window watching us," my wife said.

I focused the picture, delicately cocked the camera, and began to press the shutter release. The picture suddenly went fuzzy.

I couldn't get the cottage in focus. It was silly to be nervous, but any time you sneak up an alley like a burglar you are already nervous. And although we weren't doing anything wrong, I just wanted to get this done and over with quickly.

"Take the picture and let's go. She's *staring* at us," my wife hissed.

"But I can't!" I said. "There's something wrong with my camera. It's never done this before!"

I took my eye from the viewfinder to examine the camera. I became confused, for now the camera was out of focus.

Then I heard a "clink" on the sandy cobbles at my feet. The lens of my eyeglasses had fallen out the moment I went to snap the picture. I had not pressed it against the viewfinder to knock it out, for it had fallen forward and was resting on the viewfinder when the picture went fuzzy. That was enough for me. My wife was nervous and wanted to go. It was blistering hot, and we left without taking the shot.

The widow had been kind. It was her doing. She could not let a picture be taken of a rose that was so sacred to her, and for six years after that, neither lens fell out of those glasses again.

Now I pray that the widow rest in peace, for I am telling the story of her miraculous rosebush.

I never got a photo of the cottage, nor did anyone take pictures of the new rose each day to prove the story beyond a doubt, and unfortunately, if you go to La Ciotat today, you will find a parking lot where the widow's cottage once stood, just beyond the post office.

As I have already explained in the preface to this story, many years later, when computers had been invented, I went to type the story called "The Evil Eye" that I had written in an old notebook. But the keyboard stopped in the middle of the first sentence. After that my keyboard worked perfectly for anything else, but if I opened a new page and began to type the widow's story, it went dead. I tried this several times over several days and decided not to persist—for after all, this was about the evil eye, and I had already had a close shave.

It was many years later that I was thinking about the widow's story again and it hit me. It is a story about a work accident.

This is a story that might have been told by Greek or Roman ship workers in La Ciotat, only the equipment that caused the accident was not a giant crane or a heavy winch or a moving ship, but the evil eye itself. This was the story of an accident caused by the evil eye.

Both you and I can picture the widow's husband joyfully planting a rosebush for his wife at the corner of their little cottage, with modest hopes of covering their house with beautiful flowers. Before the day was out, however, the bush became a gift of tragedy, and in a mother's anguish, not long after, an oath was made against that gift and the man who gave it. We do not know the oath, but we can guess words spoken in the cold heat of her sorrow, and the evil eye was there to back up the oath. It was an accident, a slip of the tongue—and a word backed by the evil eye has razor-sharp blades. With the first bloom her husband died.

My keyboard kept me from telling the tale and passing it off for less than it was. Take a moment to think about what it must be like to be born with the power of the evil eye. You might think it a great gift to have the power to will things into happening, to make lenses fall from eyeglasses, to make tires or hearts burst. Others may consider it an awful misfortune. But to have the evil eye is not your choice, and if you have it and make mistakes, you must bear your mistakes with pangs of guilt.

The rosebush reminded her of that awful moment when she learned of her son's death, and her grief exploded at her husband. Yet the rosebush understood and provided a perfect bloom from beneath its crown of thorns each day. With this daily blessing she lived in peace to the end of her days.

When she died they took down her cottage along with the rosebush. All that was left of the little miracle is this story, which you are welcome to take as you will. For the world is still full of fairy tales and myths as old as Nebuchadnezzar. And if you keep your eyes and ears and minds open, you will find some of them. Then hold onto them long enough to understand them, and pray hard that you tell them properly.

Which reminds me of the double-rose in my backyard, which clearly had little to do with any of this, except that it was such a rare thing that I did a drawing of it that fits very nicely with one of the parking lot by the post office.

The Weaver's Tale

A Folk Tale That Never Was, of a Young Man's Journey from Here to There and Back Again

As told to his cousin
who might have been a weaver.

A Young Man Sets Out in the World

Once upon a time there was a patient woman who made rugs. She set her loom with complex and beautiful patterns, and sat tying hundreds and thousands of knots for weeks on end to make fine carpets. She worked at a window in a shed beside her cottage, halfway up a mountainside. From there she watched over the town and the harbor spread out below her. Through the window she also gathered gossip from all those who passed on their way over the mountain to the valleys beyond. So the woman got a reputation over the years for her wisdom.

She had a sister in the town below who had a son. And when the son became old enough to make his way in the world, he was sent to his aunt the weaver to ask about life and its meaning, in order to better prepare him for the world.

So the young man came to his aunt, and, following his mother's wishes, asked her, "What is the meaning of life?"

And his aunt replied, "I will tell you.

"Each day you should come here, and I will tell you."

"Can't I just come this once?" asked the young man, for like most kids he was impatient and wanted to get on with things.

"No, you will have to come every day," she smiled, "for if

77

you will look out there below, as I have looked all these years, you will see that it is different each day."

"The meaning of life will be different?"

"Of course," she said. "It will be different each day, and from all the answers you will weave a rug. And from this you will find the meaning of life."

"I will find the meaning from the rug?" he asked.

"No, from the weaving," she said.

"Ahhh," said her nephew. "This is good enough for me, and I think I understand. Now I can go on my way into the world."

His aunt straightened up in her seat and looked the boy in the eyes.

"Perhaps. But you cannot just ask once and expect to weave a rug from this answer. You must continue to ask tomorrow and the next day, your whole life, drawing many conclusions from the disconnected threads."

The young man scrunched up his face for a moment in thought.

"So that's how it is!" he finally said. "I guess I don't need to know the meaning of life that badly. I must go and live it."

Then his aunt smiled. "So! I see you are a weaver."

One Weaver Becomes Two and Then One Again

The young man left his aunt's workshop feeling very confident in himself, for hadn't she said he was "a weaver," and ready to live and ask questions all by himself? But he hadn't gotten far on the road when he ran into a distant cousin of his, coming back from the wars with half an arm and a twisted spine.

They got talking and went into a tavern to continue, and the young man told his cousin where he was headed and where he had come from.

"Go back to Auntie," said the soldier, "for she said you will be a weaver, and that you should be. Her rugs sell for cash, which is better than the years I have slept in holes and pigsties and bug-ridden tents."

And then the old soldier began telling him all kinds of stories of what he'd seen and done and heard about people all over the world. And this is how the weaver's story actually begins. For the boy did just what his cousin suggested. Each day he walked up the hillside from town, and each day he sat with his aunt and learned to weave, and each day she told him about something she had seen and what it meant. Very soon he was making his own rugs and selling them for a good price, and in just six years he was able to build a cottage above his aunt's shed, and everyone called that part of the road "the Weaver's Hook." I would draw you a picture of their two cottages and the shed, what with all the colored yarns dying and ovens working and overhanging trees over the dusty curve in the road. But as this book is not in color, I will draw you a picture of his cousin, instead, admonishing the young man to return to his aunt.

Go back to Auntie!

One day, not long after, news reached the town of a great army approaching from beyond the mountains with a whole nation of people in its train. No one knew where they were coming from, or what disaster had chased them from their homeland, but it was soon clear that they were making right for the pass through mountains to the sea, and that they intended to overrun the town and all its surrounding lands and take them for their own.

Now, when the weaver's aunt heard of this she said it was a shame that things happened as they did, because she was afraid there would be a bloody war, even though the land around them was large enough for ten nations of people as large as the one approaching.

"You are joking," her nephew the weaver replied, for he had never heard anything said like this before.

"Why, I am sure!" she said. "For as I weave, I stare down at the road beyond, and am often startled to see a thousand roads instead of just one. The mountains have been quarried and mined and logged and dotted with orange rooftops, and the harbor is filled with a fleet of white ships taking the wealth of this land and the products of all of our hands to other countries to sell. And where you see little houses with one or two families, I have seen tall straight castles with thousands of families in them."

The young man's eyes bugged out to hear this, because it was surely a vision of things to come.

And she continued, "I have already told the city fathers to welcome this people and not to oppose them. But I know the city fathers. One is my brother and your uncle, and they are already preparing for war. My brother would rather lose everything than share anything. I must go to meet these people beyond the mountains and tell them my vision. For there is enough for all in this place of ours, and they should come and offer peace.

"I'm an old woman whom they cannot fear. If I don't come back in eight days you must run away and hide—for they will have killed me, and they will kill you, too."

"*Auntie please!*" The young weaver pleaded. "You must escape with the rest of us now!"

She winced.

"I'm sorry. I continue to hope for a more just and thoughtful world, even though I expect stupidity and selfishness. If I don't try to stop this war, I will only have stupidity and selfishness to hope for, and that is not hope."

Then she tied herself to her donkey and trotted up the mountain path, over the pass, and down to the valley where the warrior nation was advancing.

The wise woman was killed very quickly by an advance patrol on horseback before she could even deliver her message. A soldier had made a bet with his buddy that his blade was sharp enough to cut the next person to come by in half with one stroke. So when the aunt's donkey returned to the young man with her feet still in the stirrups, he escaped into the mountains, and this is how it came about that the weaver set out into the world.

... with her feet still in the stirrups.

The Weaver and the Fisherman

There once was a young weaver who was wandering the world. His family and his teacher were slaughtered by an invading people. The people would have been welcomed into the weaver's land, for it was a rich land, and many farmers and workers and sailors were needed by the city fathers, who like city fathers everywhere were overflowing with generosity and good will. But the invaders never stopped to ask anything of anyone before they came, and so destroyed everything.

As the weaver wandered he met merchants and holy men and innkeepers, and farmers, soldiers, and women of the world, and would tell each of them this story and ask how people could be so stupid and shortsighted—how instead of building a great future they chose to destroy the very workshops and farms and fleets that would have made them prosperous and happy.

Everyone told him his story was nothing, and then recited all the evils they had suffered or seen. Everyone had a story. But all the stories didn't help the young weaver much at all, and often angered him the more; and so he wandered on.

One day he heard of a wise fisherman who lived in a hut above a mountain lake. Despite misgivings at meeting just another old man whom common folk supposed wise, the weaver went to him and told his story. Finally he asked, "Why must people remain vain, shortsighted, and arrogant?"

"You must come back tomorrow," the fisherman began, "and I will tell you one reason ..."

"And must I return the next day to learn the second reason?" added the young man, for he was familiar with this game of wisdom.

The fisherman smiled.

"From these I will show you how to tie them together into another reason. And each day you can tie a new one, for there are as many reasons for mankind's stupidity and shortsightedness as there are knots in my net."

"So I see," exclaimed the young man. "You have told me enough. For it has already been clear to me that self-indulgence is the first reason, and laziness—a form of self-indulgence—is the second. And from these two failings I can weave the entire net of human stupidity, short-sightedness, arrogance, and all the rest."

"So you came with your answer prepared, I see," the fishman piped up. "Even so, you must come again tomorrow, as I said, to make sure you understand your answer."

The weaver stared at the fisherman.

"Come *back*? But I've already unraveled the knot—I no longer have a problem."

The fisherman smiled a sly grin. "And so? You have told me how my net is woven. Of what use is that to you? Go! A net is no use if you don't know how and where to cast it."

"But you are not so wise, old man," replied the youth, "for perhaps I don't wish to use my net to catch fish in their folly. For this net may catch fish, but it also lets justice pass through it.

"We can catch fish, and we can be caught—but you see, I was looking for justice, which cannot be caught in *your* net."

The fisherman was smiling a broad smile now.

"You didn't ask me for justice," he grinned, slyly.

But the weaver only continued: "And perhaps it is I who am in the water—and want the net to keep the fools out. I know just where to cast my net—and you are on the other side!"

Suddenly he stopped and caught himself.

"And you?" he asked, suddenly feeling embarrassed. "If you are truly a fisherman, do you know how to catch men at their folly?"

The fisherman winked. "I see that at least you are not a rogue," he said.

"And I would like to believe you are not one either," said the young man. "So I will go back to weaving, like my old teacher." But as he turned to go, he graciously added, "Like you, yourself."

For the fisherman had never stopped mending his nets, and the weaver felt ashamed of himself. For before he had come, he knew he would be matching wits, and in playing that game he had succumbed to arrogance.

As he turned, the fisherman broke into a hearty laugh.

I have certainly been caught in that net of his, the young man thought. Yet he was surprised to see the old man holding a fishing pole, chortling and shaking it as if he had just hooked a big fish.

So indeed it had been a game.

The weaver bowed his head, took off his belt, and put it in his mouth. Then he led himself up to the fisherman, whose glee only increased at seeing the weaver's way of admitting defeat.

... Chortling and shaking it as if he had hooked a big fish

The old man jumped down from his step and embraced the young weaver.

"I hoped you would come back. You are no ordinary fish. Your teacher is very proud, now."

Then the weaver spoke. "Only one line is necessary to catch a fish, and my own self-indulgence was enough to catch me."

The fisherman smiled back. "We have both learned something, eh?"

"Something deep down tells us there is only one answer, and even I, who struggled for wisdom, attempted to prove I had it," admitted the weaver.

The fisherman re-lit his pipe.

"I haven't enjoyed myself so much for a long time," he said.

"When you played me at the game of wise man I took you up on it, but began to feel foolish indeed. When I saw you had caught yourself, it was very amusing."

The young weaver sat down, a bit uneasily. For by acting the know-it-all just that once, he had become arrogant—like the men he could not forgive. Understanding this, he had to forgive them all, yet he was queasy about it, nevertheless.

"Yes," said the fisherman, "those the world often calls 'wise' look at the world around them as if it is the answer. They spend their lives exploring it with many challenges.

"Yet every man and woman has the ultimate answer. Even if they don't succeed, they rarely have to change their answer for long. Their purpose is to find that their own life meets the challenge of nature, that what they know and who they are is good enough."

The fisherman stopped a moment and shook his head sadly.

"Those who humbly seek after knowledge look for the challenges that answer their questions of life, and those who simply live take on the challenge every day. It is human nature to feel we have an answer to everything."

At this, both the fisherman and the young weaver sat down on the old stone wall and paused. For it was a disturbing thought that we cannot stop arrogant behavior by learning. All of us will be the source of ignorant actions because we have the source of all answers within us. It is part of every spirit to have the answers, and we are bound—every so often (or all the time)—to act that way.

They sat there many hours sharing a smoke and stories of what they'd seen and things they'd heard about, and what it all might mean. And of course, this is one of those stories.

The Sailor

A weaver once lived with a fisherman by the shore of a lake. They were fast friends and talked about many things. In the winter the lake became frozen solid and covered with snow, perfectly flat and quite fine for a battle.

That winter, two enemy armies converged on the lake to decide who was the strongest.

The fisherman and the weaver took up a hiding place in a tree. Soon the armies clashed and fought a massive and bloody battle on the ice. Those who were left alive got away; but those left behind putrefied under the bright winter sun—and with the coming of spring the ice melted and the foul gore of horses and men sank into the water and poisoned it, so there could be no more fishing in that lake for many, many years.

The weaver and the fisherman packed up the fisherman's nets and began a trek down to the sea. When they got to a small seaport they noticed a young boy readying the rigging of a vessel below them in port. They watched as the boy finished his work and swam ashore.

As he walked past the two men the weaver addressed him: "I see you can tie knots."

"I tie the best of all my brothers and cousins," the boy replied.

"You will be a clever man," said the fisherman. "Is there good fishing in these parts?"

"Not here," said the boy. "The fish aren't so plentiful. The men fish beyond the far islands."

"Perhaps they should mend their nets," said the old man. "They might catch more. For I have never fished the sea, but then I have never seen nets with more holes in them than these. I can mend the very worst of nets."

"Our nets never wear out," said the boy.

"Perhaps we should weave sailcloth, then," said the weaver.

"We always have many extra sails of the best and strongest cloth," said the boy.

"So what is a man to do?" asked the fisherman.

"Why," said the boy, "a man cannot trust the current, but must always seek out the slightest winds and sail them. This is what my father always tells me and my brothers. This is what a man is to do."

"I think your father may be a wise man," said the weaver. "We should meet with him, for the both of us are quite becalmed. There's no wind, just currents taking us from one place to another."

So they went to the café where the boy's father was drinking and playing checkers. They chatted a while, and then the old fisherman sighed, "What gives a man the courage to start over? Where do we get the energy to go on?"

The boy's father lifted a glass. "This evening, with this drink in my hand, I will give you one reason," said the sailor. "And tomorrow night you can buy me another drink and I'll tell you another."

"And how many months must we fill your cup?" laughed the weaver.

"As many days as there are clouds up in the sky!" returned the sailor. "For there are as many things that drive us to do what we do as there are clouds that drive the winds.

"They say there are four winds, but they are wrong. There aren't even forty—but hundreds of different winds. And I would show you them, but we would need a lifetime. And each one, you play against your sails a different way, depending on how it strikes you and which way you wish to go."

The fisherman sat back and drew a long puff from his pipe. "This is only too true. But how about when there is no wind?"

"Play checkers," answered the sailor.

"So I see."

"And when you are becalmed far from the shore?"

"Pray, and then take out your checkers."

"And if you had no checkers?"

The sailor grinned a big toothy smile, "I might die."

"Is it worth buying you all these drinks, then?"

"Not at all. For as soon as there's a wind," said the sailor, "you should have to drink them yourself! I'll be many miles from here!"

"I know something of sailing," replied the fisherman. "And your answer sounded true enough for a moment. You certainly spoke of the wind as spirit, as a sailor's breath. And the spirit must move you from without—from within you can only keep it alive by praying and playing."

"But what if you cut down the sails?" struck up the weaver.

The sailor downed his drink and poured everyone another.

"Now there's a subject for you! There are a hundred ways to set a man adrift. By loosening his sails, or fraying his cordage, or ..."

"Or breaking off his keel?" The old fisherman frowned. "For a man with no keel may row, perhaps, and might take a tail-wind, but with no fiber or morals, he'll hold no strong wind. He loses spirit the moment it moves him. To move a mile he must tack twelve more, from this side to that. With no keel on the broad ocean, can you keep your sights straight without losing your way?"

The sailor grew silent.

"It's true. You have spoken well. There are too many of us with no keel at all, even though we play at being the best and fastest sailors. We tack and go nowhere."

He stood up and looked to the door.

"The sailors in this town have always traded in precious cargoes—slaves and weapons and stolen goods. But many of us got tired of being middlemen. We said, 'why pay for a cargo when we can take it for a good fight and a few dead?' As smugglers we risked the same fate. We were outside of the law and could be killed for it. So why not be pirates and killers ourselves?"

"When I saw the state of your nets I guessed right," sighed the fisherman. "But what of your town, your families? You cannot have it both ways, to be both pirates and family men."

"You asked how a man may keep going, cut off from the world. Here is your answer." He began to pace, saying nothing. But seeing him pace nervously, the few other men in the café got up to leave. The coffee house was soon empty except for the three men and the boy.

"We played the winds with no thought of tomorrow, with no thought of consequences. And now our town is surrounded— the navies of four states are slowly herding our ships back into port. They will be here by tomorrow morning. We were to have slipped past them tonight."

The sailor flung himself down in his chair and covered his head.

"As you see, I'm not just playing checkers." He didn't look up as he poured himself another drink.

His son looked startled. He began looking around the café as if any moment the enemy would break in. Suddenly he looked at his father, mouth agape. He understood. He ran for the door and bolted home as fast as he could to tell his mother and brothers. He had been readying his father's sails for an escape, but his father had never intended to take them at all. They would all have been killed! They must escape while there was time!

The fisherman and the weaver quietly got up from their chairs and began to leave. The sailor jumped to his feet and blocked their way.

"Our families knew we were leaving tonight, but not why. We're all murderers. To save our necks we would have left our families, believing that perhaps they'd be spared. To stay and defend them, we would *all* have been slaughtered.

"There is no good way. When a man is cut from the spirit he's a husk. Everyone pays his debts. He may as well be dead.

"So, *here* is your answer!" He pulled a short two-edged dirk from his belt.

"Sails we had—but only to run away. And *now* you know."

His throat seemed to thicken and his nostrils flared wide.

"But I'll let you know something else about the men of this town—*we will kill.*" His eyes blazed as he thrust the knife with both hands deep, up into his lungs, "ke-eell to ke-e-ep our ke-e-el!"

He laughed at this last spark of wit. Then he barked, coughed, and fell over on the table.

The weaver and the fisherman found a back door and left the café unseen. As dusk turned to moonlight they passed by way of the marshes and hid themselves in the reeds on a dry rise of land. When morning came the horizon glowed with flames and plumes of smoke. Many other families had been alerted by the sailor's son, and escaped with them into the marshes. The enemy had contented itself with destroying the town and its ships. Even so, those who had escaped lived for several days on raw clams. They didn't dare light a fire.

"I think pirates enjoy melodrama," said the weaver as they finally packed up to leave. "He could have helped his family escape as we did."

"Perhaps," answered the fisherman. "And if they had mended their nets they would have caught fish and never needed to escape."

And so it was that the two began to carefully pick their way out of the bog into the misty moors that stretched to the horizon.

The Stray

There were once two friends who had traveled to a town to find work, only to find the population fleeing because it was about to be sacked.

After several days on the road, they began to realize they were among the homeless, starting each day with no certain direction, looking to each stopping place as a possible refuge and place to settle down and get work. Both friends had trades, for one was a journeyman weaver and the other was a fisherman and net-maker, with many years of experience.

After several days on the road it began to rain very hard, and they took cover under a stone bridge. As the day went on, many other travelers joined them. They became aware of a very ragged old crone poking around, as if to turn over stones—but really to peek at everyone's bags, and maybe poke into some bags in the bargain.

The expression carved into the lines of her face was without guile. She was not sneaky. Her face betrayed no thoughts at all, and if you had caught her stealing, you might have simply taken your belongings back and given her a push. People's belongings were like rocks to be turned over, under which something might be discovered—an olive, a dried kipper, a broken piece of cheese. Certainly not money. She looked like she wouldn't recognize it, anyway.

As she passed the weaver's bags he sat bolt upright and grabbed the end of her stick.

"You!" he laughed. "I have a question for you. If you can hear and can speak my language, that is."

The woman didn't respond. Immobile, as if she had been there all along, a part of the background, she didn't pull her stick away but let the weaver hold it.

The weaver turned to the fisherman. "Sharp as an auger. If she speaks, she will untie many of our knots, old man."

The fisherman studied the old woman carefully. Her eyes stared at nothing in particular; she breathed with no apparent anxiety, and stood as if asleep—as if she were between time.

In fact, the weaver had caught time, not her. She only waited for time to begin again.

The fisherman took out a small rug and laid it out.

"My friend here is a weaver," he began. "His aunt helped him make his very first rug.

"A rug is spread before a man's hearth. Here, these men have lit a fire, and would be honored should you remain in our little corner of this world."

The weaver looked at the woman and then looked around at the scattered leftovers of families and farms, the world of a fishermen and a weaver huddled together under a bridge. He began to retell their story, and spoke of how each time a deep question was asked, the answer was given to them—but only to miss something just as deep—a most important something.

As the weaver talked, the old lady's eyes began to move, as if she were following things in a dream. But when the story was over, the old crone just stood there motionless, without a word.

He tugged at her stick a bit.

"Woman! Can you speak? What is your name? Where are you from?"

"Let her go on her way," said the fisherman. "I don't believe she will want to talk about much."

And so the weaver let go of her stick, and the moment he did, the old woman began shuffling along and poking stones and people's bags as if nothing had happened. After a little bit, however, she began poking and shuffling in place—turning around and around. Then she stopped poking and shuffled over to the rug between the weaver and the fisherman and squatted down.

"I am Therese," she said. "I am the rat catcher's daughter. I live at the big river by the miller's cottage. You were talking about …" She paused.

"I was," smiled the weaver.

"I have a rug like this one, and a big house. I have a big house." She seemed reflective. "I live in a big house with cows. Herds of cows, you know. Herds of cows in my big house. Sheep. I watch sheep good." She looked earnestly at both men.

"In the cellar, in the stove, cows, pots, forks—cows everywhere. Can *you help* me?"

The fisherman smiled at the weaver and looked through his sack. He gave the woman a heel of bread and some smoked fish, which she ripped apart into pieces that she stuffed in her mouth.

"I am sailing around the world now on a ship. It's my father's ship. He brought it here yesterday. It's over there, by the miller's cottage."

"My dear lady," asked the fisherman, "do you fish?"

"Yes. I have never eaten a fish. Never."

She looked up with a pious-looking face at the weaver. "Can you *help* me?"

The weaver turned to the fisherman.

"I would like to help this lady, sir. Would you mind if I gave her our rug, here?"

"Not at all," said the fisherman. "It is yours, madam. And when the rain stops, if you wish, you may join us as far as the next town."

The old lady simply stared into space for a long time. The

weaver and fisherman said nothing and pretended to go to sleep. Finally she squatted down on the rug and went to sleep, just like that.

"She is completely cut off from life, and keeps living," said the weaver. "I believe she has been brought to us as an answer."

"I would not have guessed it," said the fisherman. "She is a human cork—with no sails and no keel, cast here and there. Yet she lives with only remnants of a human spirit."

The weaver shook his head.

"She's a stray. She created a world with words that had only vague meanings. The cows and sheep and the house with a fireplace have no connection to any part of her. She grabbed for words to make conversation only to please us. Her plea for help was only recalling days when she spoke with other humans. This woman has lived in silence for many years."

Early the next morning the dew began to collect and the pair awoke before dawn. The woman was already up, and she puttered around in small circles so as not to lose her new hosts, who she had remembered meant food.

The two got up and on their way. The old woman was scurrying back and forth across the path in all directions at their rear, poking at bushes and kicking at immobile crickets and hidden lizards.

"She is quite like a stray. With half as much wit, I'm afraid," observed the weaver.

"I wonder why I ever thought she could answer us anything."

"Wait until tonight. Perhaps we can get her to talk again."

And so the two walked on, gently reminding the old lady of their direction every once in a while. And when they sat to eat, she would stand a way off until they invited her to join them. When she had her food she would take it to a secluded spot and eat alone. But when night came and they prepared to bed down, the old lady disappeared. The two didn't appear to worry and went about their business, for everyone has befriended a stray, and knows they can be trusted to take care of themselves—and sometimes to befriend you in turn.

They talked a while and then lay down to sleep. Suddenly the weaver realized there was something poking around at his bag. He grabbed the old lady's stick, just as he had the night before.

"I think this lady here has the answer to our problems!" he said, imitating his voice from the night before.

And so they repeated their first meeting with the old lady. And they did so on each successive night. And each night their ritual ended with some questioning of the old lady.

Just as the weaver thought, she had forgotten her speech after long disuse. So as each day turned into the next, she remembered a little more and her talk became more coherent. And as it did, she wandered around less and less as they walked, and seemed to tag along behind them listening for any stray conversation that might leave their lips. It was as if speech bound her to them— even their slightest observations along the road, and the smallest gossip about those they had met or seen on their travels.

Slowly, too, they learned her story—which was not especially remarkable. She was a rat catcher's daughter. She and her mother were thrown out of the town when her father was first to die of the plague. And thus they began wandering. Yet the whole town died, and it was they who were spared. They worked at inns here and there, until her mother was burned in a kitchen accident and died—but Therese had a lame arm from childhood, and she could not earn her keep alone. So she had been a wandering beggar ever since her mother died, and the many adventures that others might have recounted of those years were no more than a single long walk in her mind.

"It is remarkable," the weaver said one night, "for my aunt observed so much over her years, just sitting at her loom. She became serene with her lot, and wise in many ways. Yet Therese has observed the world far longer. She is old enough to have lived in the old empire, but what has she gained by it?"

The old lady turned. "I met his highness, the Emperor."

And this is how the weaver and the fisherman heard the old woman's story.

The Old Woman's Story

Once upon a time there was an old woman who stood with a crooked cane and told her story to two travelers—a fisherman and a weaver.

"I was married to the Emperor when I was a young girl," she said, smiling and staring at the two men as if they were somewhere far away.

"He came to our inn one afternoon, on his way to a war. We were married that night. All the singing and drinking! All the food! It was the biggest day. And then they went away to fight. The Emperor told me he would be gone a long time, but he would never forget me and would return for me one day. That was the biggest day of my life 'til now, for he is coming for me today."

The weaver and the fisherman looked at each other and smiled to hear the old woman. She had walked with them for many weeks, and they had come to love her as if she were an aunt they shared. As she told them this story, they were not surprised to see tears in each other's eyes.

She continued to speak.

"The two men who stayed had swords. They said if I ever said anything they would find out and come and kill me and my mother. They had sharp oiled swords. They were very bad men!"

Then her eyes focused, and she became conscious of the weaver and the fisherman. She began to tremble.

"I have told the secret that I am the Emperor's wife and now you are here to kill me! It is *you!* You tricked me and are going to kill me, for I have told!"

Wild-eyed with terror, she turned and started to run. For several steps she leapt as if her feet had forgotten she had grown old. Then she stumbled and fell, and began getting up, looking back in fear.

But the exertion was too much. She let out a sigh and clutched her chest and fell over. When the weaver reached her, her eyes were already rolling back, as in death. There was no breath, and her lids were heavy and closing.

Suddenly her eyes opened. She gasped for breath. She saw the weaver and felt him holding her. She smiled impishly.

"I was wrong. You didn't come to kill me. You came back to tell me he's coming. I see him there! My husband is coming for me now! His Highness the Emperor is coming, just now, I see him!"

Her eyes were beaming, her smile was radiant. She watched expectantly as the fisherman walked slowly toward them both. Her smile seemed to glow with a radiant happiness as he approached. The fisherman understood that she must be dying, and he leaned over, and held her shoulders tightly, and kissed her sweetly on the forehead. Then he closed her eyes. A very old lady had passed away, and she was blushing.

An Empty Farmhouse

Once upon a time there were two friends. One was a weaver and one was a fisherman. The two had walked many miles together when they came on an old woman in the road who was very near death, and they stayed with her and comforted her as if she were one of them, a very old friend. She died very peacefully, believing she was with her husband and the family whom she had lost many years before.

Her name was Therese, and when she died the two men wrapped her body in a blanket, and put it in some bushes and set off to the closest farm to borrow a shovel and perhaps an extra hand to help them dig her grave and say a novena. For neither the fisherman nor the weaver knew their prayers, but they thought it only right that they should provide their new friend a proper burial.

The closest farm was visible from where they stood, beyond fields of sunflowers. The high road had come through a small glen and common forest, where the townspeople cut their wood, and a village sat on a hillside, with walls of a castle tower rising above it.

As they approached the farm they could smell smoke from the hearth and see lights burning, but when they knocked at the door and called, no one responded. They walked all around the farmhouse and even saw food on the table, but not a soul around.

"This is very strange," said the weaver.

"But we have seen stranger," replied the fisherman. "Let us leave them a note that we will borrow two shovels from the loft and return them shortly. These people wouldn't deny an old lady a proper burial."

They did this and walked back to the old lady named Therese.

"Let us dig," said the fisherman, "and while we do I will tell you the story of the Swan."

The weaver gave him a strange look.

"How is it that suddenly you have found another story in your mind that you haven't already told me all these many months we have been together?" the weaver asked the fisherman.

"The Swan's Tale came to me when we passed that brook on the way," the fisherman answered. "I saw a swan in the shadows, and thought I'd never thought much about these birds. I always found them to be empty and arrogant, with a long curved neck fashioned to look at their own reflection. Always preening, never doing anything of consequence, a swan just seemed the 'finishing touch' of a pretty and peaceful landscape. Just so. Just so, when it is part of a landscape we forget it is a bird."

"But you said your swan was in the shadows."

"Ah yes," the fisherman reflected. "The landscape was missing. And so I simply saw a giant bird. Did you know a swan can fly? Every now and then on my lake I would see them. For when a swan flies it is a powerful, majestic, and awe-inspiring sight."

And so the fisherman told the story of a man called "the Swan."

The Swan

Once upon a time there were two friends who had walked many miles together. They came on an old woman in the road who was very near death, and they stayed with her and comforted her as if they were old friends. And she died very peacefully, believing she was with her husband and the family whom she had lost many years before.

After she died the men went to a farmhouse to find a shovel to dig her a grave and give her proper burial. But when they got to the farmhouse they found it recently abandoned, for there was no one about, and no horses in the stables. But there was the smell of bread still baking, and there was corn just poured in the horses' troughs. And so after much consideration, they borrowed shovels and returned to the road where the old lady was lying.

Now it happened that the hills nearby were well known for brigands, and that this part of the road where the old lady had died was always carefully watched, for the townspeople were on guard for brigands. Seeing what had taken place, with two men standing over a body by the road, the farmer and his family had taken off in great haste to the village and its castle on the hillside.

So that just as soon as the men had buried the old lady, they heard the sounds of approaching hoofs on the evening breeze, and a squadron of dragoons from the castle soon surrounded them and they were arrested and led off in shackles to the castle.

The two were hustled down the steps into the castle's dungeon, and shoved brusquely into a new world, far from any thoughts of their previous freedom. They caught a whiff of the dank cold air and heard the clank of iron gates behind them. Then a voice politely asked of their health from somewhere in the darkness."

"Thank you," replied the fisherman, "we are in the best of health, but in the most regrettable circumstance."

"You must be the Swan," said the weaver impatiently, "for my friend here has promised me the story of a man called 'the Swan' and I would like the story to proceed swiftly to its conclusion, as it might see us out of jail."

At this the fisherman winked at the weaver for his cleverness, but it was too dark for the weaver to see.

This caused the weaver to laugh.

"I see you were listening," the fisherman said.

"I certainly was," said the weaver. "In *both* cases. Please continue!"

So the fisherman went on with his story about a man called "the Swan."

"Yes, I am called the Swan," the voice said. "But what of it? I no longer regret being here. What I hate is being taken out on display, for my eyes can't see in that light, and children throw dirt and pebbles at me, until soon all the villagers throw clods of muck and garbage on me. This I regret."

"Why are you on display?" the fisherman asked.

"You, too, will be on display, next festival day, which is the day after tomorrow I've been told. It is the only way I count time."

"I don't understand," said the weaver.

"The more the people hate the prince the more dung they

will heap on you, mark my words. It is the only thing he gives them on these festivals—free dried horse manure and soggy trash to throw."

"Why are you here?" the weaver asked.

"I suppose it is because I was freer than the rest of them."

"But that is nonsense, and unjust."

"Perhaps it is neither. Perhaps it is true," said the Swan. "For I am still freer than they."

"How long have they kept you here?!" the weaver asked.

"What is the difference?" the prisoner answered. "My freedom is due to a peculiar blessing. I have no real recollection of time at all except for festival days, and yet here in this darkness I remember all of my thoughts, and I am free to choose what I think and think what I choose.

"Out there, I thought of nothing but the world I was witnessing. I soon became what I saw, for I watched horrified as innocents were sacrificed, and was soon doing it myself. In the light, my soul had descended to darkness. In this darkness I have been graced with light, for I never bother to think the same thing again, and only seem to remember my blessings, which come to me in a different way each day. Today they brought me two fellow prisoners. Today I have the joy to speak. And soon I can be quiet, for I don't wish to say the same things twice."

"This is very interesting and quite noble of you," said the fisherman. "I could have hardly guessed that a swan thinks so many new thoughts as it glides around on the water staring at itself."

"Today neither the farmer nor the duke is as free as I am. But that isn't the reason for my name, for to glide on the water looking at oneself is hardly different than most people in this world. Nevertheless I will tell you my tale, for to me it seems to have happened long ago to someone else.

"There was a young man who was about to get married. Before the wedding his friends took him to the tavern to celebrate, where he got drunk. When he awoke he found he had enlisted in the king's dragoons, and was on his way to the armory to get his saber and musket and plumed helmet and stripes on his sleeves. He was saddened but not so upset by this turn of events, for it seemed he had woken up from one dream to be placed into another.

"He was sent for training, where he swore service to the king each day, and heard many ugly things about the king's enemies. It seemed he had never heard such ugly things in his life.

"Soon he was sent into service, where he was honored and won medallions for his valor. He often won ribbons for killing old men and women who protected their sons and daughters in their homes, and for killing any captives who cried out as they were led from the battlefield. He began to forget how many people he'd killed, and came to hate them all. When the king decreed that children spread the pox and must be killed, he was the first to do the hated deed and win his ribbons. But soon his eyes became vacant and he cared for nothing, neither medals nor ribbons. It was all the officers' business and the king's war. When his twenty years of service were up he left the king's army and went home.

"When he got to his village it seemed as if everyone had been killed and a new town had moved in. Yet he knew everyone and everyone knew him. Both his parents were alive and overjoyed to have him back. Yet it was as if they were among dead of the villages he had burned. His fiancée was since married and widowed, yet the soldier saw her with empty eyes and she was nowhere to be found among the living. So he sadly took up residence above the tavern and sat each day at a table on the square staring into his beer, trying to remember who all these people were and who he was.

"One day he sat at his bench outside the tavern. The storekeeper's son was kicking stones in the square. He had often seen this boy, but today he recognized him. He saw a boy, a living boy; and then he heard the sound of a lark. A breeze carried the smell of wet hay from the fields, now mixed with sausages grilling from inside the tavern. These were the smells and sounds of the soldier's childhood.

"At that moment some dragoons rode into town, and one fellow, the closest, reminded the old soldier of a young version of himself. The boy, too, saw their uniforms and shining sabers and recognized himself all grown-up. He ran to make his best kick, to send a little stone, his best kick ever, to the fountain! But he slipped and the cobble bounced into the dragoon's horse, which reared, and almost unsaddled the dragoon. After calming his horse, the dragoon dismounted and began beating the boy with a rod, 'til the storekeeper rescued his son with a blow to the dragoon's chin. The dragoon got up and ran the storekeeper through with his sword. Several villagers in the store and the square ran at the dragoon with their knives drawn. The rest of the squadron had by this time dismounted at the inn and looked around to see what had kept their mate. Seeing he was in trouble, they jumped to their horses and drew their sabers, preparing to mow the villagers down like wheat.

"But as they mounted, the old retired soldier felt something he had never felt in his life come over him. He leapt from his beer and pulled the last dragoon from his horse, grabbed his sword, mounted his horse and charged into the rear of the squadron like a madman, killing all of them with the energy it takes to swat flies.

"After that he fled to the next kingdom, for he'd become a bandit. Those who saw him kill an entire squadron named him 'the Swan.' They said his sword flew through his enemies with the power and splendor of a swan's wings in flight. He had simply been part of the landscape for years, simply sitting in the same seat, staring into his beer.

"When the Swan made it over the border into the enemy's kingdom he thought himself safe. But war, you should know, is the best way to keep a people united under you if you have nothing else to give them, and so it turned out that the two enemy kings were in fact the very best friends. So the Swan was immediately arrested and sent back over the border to jail.

"He was put into the dungeon of a prince who had few friends, far from the Swan's own village where his story was well-known. There, on festival days, the local prince would put him in chains and have him paraded before the people, who loved spectacles and fun, for they might throw off their misery for a few moments, free to degrade and humiliate those worse off than themselves. In this way the prince flummoxed their understanding of who was bad and who was good.

"Many years passed in this way, and several days before a festival, two new prisoners were thrown into the Swan's dungeon, which is where the story began."

The Swan concluded, "I have little more to tell you, and so you must leave me alone to think until the next festival comes."

"That we will do," said the weaver and the fisherman together, adding, "and we are very grateful to hear your story."

A week later the jailers entered the dungeon and connected the three prisoners to a long chain, by which they led them out. They were put on a cart and taken to the town square with fanfares and flags, as rotten eggs and soggy clods of manure pelted the captives. When they stopped the wagon to move the three prisoners to the big wooden yoke, the guards were already in a jovial mood. It was a holiday, and meant to be a good time for all. They reveled in each good throw someone made, as a clod of wet manure or rotten garbage made its mark.

It should be clear that these were times which the guards could talk about for weeks to come. And because they did this every few months they were less than vigilant about where they placed the prisoners and whether they put their weapons down. Which is how the Swan caught the right moment to catch the closest guard off his guard and strangle him with his chains. In another moment he grabbed the sledgehammer used to open the big yoke and with it he broke the chains binding his feet and connecting him to the other prisoners. Before the other soldiers could reach him he had leapt back onto the cart swinging his sledge clean across their shoulders. Suddenly the people remembered themselves. The spell was broken, and the crowd turned their fury on the soldiers, as the Swan hammered the heads off his old comrades-in-arms for the king.

Meanwhile, the weaver and the fisherman took the keys from their jailer (who had little brains left to deny them), released their chains, and made their way to the town gate. As they escaped they heard a barrage of musket fire. Given the groans and screams of the crowd immediately following, they knew the Swan and many others were now dead.

The fisherman turned to the weaver.

"That is the end of my story about the Swan."

"I should hope so," said the Weaver. "It was not extremely pleasant, but I am glad it turned out all right for you and me."

Then they lowered their friend Therese, still wrapped in the weaver's blanket, into her grave. They said prayers for her as her mother and father would, and as they were filling in the grave, the sounds of hoofs of a squadron of horses was carried in the evening breeze.

The weaver's eyes bugged out wide. The fisherman had never before let him know he could see the future.

"So it was true, after all?" the weaver asked.

"Of course," answered the fisherman. "There is some part of *all* of our stories that is true."

"I'm certainly glad you had us escape in that last part, then!"

But then the weaver grinned, for it had all become very clear. The fisherman took a big puff of his pipe. The smoke billowed out into the soft night summer air. For you see, they were still sitting and swapping stories at the fisherman's cottage, and it was simply another part of the tale the fisherman had made up, for *this* is why the fisherman had such a reputation for being so wise.

And the young weaver sat and stared over the waters of the

lake, and asked if indeed it would soon be polluted and barren. And the fisherman's answer was only, "It is up to you."

Then the weaver stared out in deep thought. He looked out at the few years behind him and the many he hoped to see, very thoughtfully, which is just as you should look at them.

For in fact he was sitting at the tavern with his cousin. The story of the fisherman was his cousin's story, as were all the other adventures we have heard—all for the price of a stein of beer. And this is because the old soldier with half an arm and a twisted spine wanted to make sure his younger cousin understood the kinds of things he might expect to see if he should set out in the world.

The young man stared at his cousin with wide and tearful eyes. "Yes. Oh my God in heaven above! It *is* up to me alone. And if you have learned and seen so much by going off to the wars, by sleeping on the ground, by the pain and suffering of half an arm and a twisted back …

"If you have seen so much to tell me such stories, then I was right all along. I will go out and *live* my life!"

So the young man embraced his cousin, and wished him the very best: "Give all my love to Auntie," the young man said to his worn-out old cousin. "She is a wonderful woman. May she live to be a hundred! And may she always follow her heart!"

But after a moment's reflection he turned about and took up his cousin's pack. For, thinking it all over, he changed his mind and decided he would walk with him back to town, live with his aunt, and learn to weave. There was so very much to weave.

Breinigsville, PA USA
09 February 2010

232233BV00001B/15/P